FAIR PLAY

by

Tracy A. Ward

FAIR PLAY
By Tracy A. Ward

Second Edition 2016
Manufactured in the United States of America

Visit Tracy's website at www.TracyAWard.com.
Copyediting and Formatting by
    www.Top-ePublishingServices.com
Cover by Sweet 'N Spicy Designs

ISBN for print version: 978-0-9972827-0-2
ISBN for eBook version: 978-0-9972827-1-9

AUTHOR'S PERSONAL NOTE

Many thanks goes to Entangled Publishing's Indulgence imprint, where the first edition of this novel was originally offered in June, 2013. Fair Play is now available by the author in its second edition as New Adult genre romantic fiction. Hope you enjoy.

CHAPTER ONE

Ashlyn

Sitting on a ladder-backed barstool at the Double Shot, still sweaty from spending the day shut up in my oven for an apartment—who didn't have AC in Texas?—I took a slug of my gin and tonic and glanced at my watch for the eight billionth time. Seven p.m. Anxiety sat like gathered fieldstone in my stomach, all jagged and sharp-edged. Lucas Marshall was late—and given the terse voice message he'd left on my cell an hour before, telling me to meet him in ten minutes, I was naturally concerned.

As the owner of The Marshall Theater, an old limestone playhouse that was both a historic landmark and one of the most prestigious regional theaters in the country, Lucas had taken a chance on me, a playwright without a hit to my name in this type of a venue, to write three original scripts for The Marshall Theater Players.

The most noteworthy thing I'd done before was help pull a small community playhouse in Arlington out of a slump. The Marshall Theater was big-time in the world of a playwright.

The Marshall Theater Players, where Lucas was also Executive and Artistic Director, performed every year at the nationally renowned Phair Theater Festival. From producers to directors, fans to critics, people swarmed the small, Texas hill country town of Phair, for the festival, hoping to discover the theater world's next big thing. The Marshall Theater Players always brought back the big wins.

A great review of my upcoming script could give me my first real shot at Broadway.

I washed down my anxiety with the dregs of the gin and tonic and pushed the empty glass across the mahogany bar. Then I nodded to Babs, the bartender. A thin wisp of a woman with bottle-black hair and too much eyeliner for someone on the upper end of fifty, Babs Blake had been a bartender with the Double Shot chain for years. She was nice enough, and friendly. Though neither of us were Phair natives, I'd actually known her since I was in high school. She'd been there for me once when I'd needed a friend. When I'd first arrived at Phair, it had been a nice welcome to see a familiar face.

"You hangin' in there, Ashlyn?" Babs asked in her clipped, New York dialect. "You look stressed."

I blew out a long breath before answering. "Waiting on Lucas and trying to keep my nerves under control." I looked around the bar. Limestone walls were decorated, all depicting the Double Shot's sixty-year history, beginning with its flagship bar in New York and ending with its most recent addition in Phair, Texas, which opened nearly eighteen months ago.

With the exception of a few guys and their wives holding court in front of the big screen, a place that had the capacity for at least a hundred and fifty sat mostly empty. I glanced outside. The wide-paned front windows gave an unobstructed view to Main Street's old-world western façade. Like the bar, the street, too, was empty. "Where is everybody?"

Babs replaced my drink before taking a drag on her electronic cigarette, the skin around her mouth puckering. "Business is slow when the theater's dark."

"That'll change in a few weeks, once people arrive for the festival." I fiddled with my stir stick. "Which means this is the calm before the storm, right?"

"Blessing and a curse." She took another drag on her e-cig. "Listen, sweetie, I heard you got a few bad reviews on your last two scripts. Those critics, they're just trying to mess with your head. You're a good writer. Don't let those bastards get to you."

To date, fifteen of the plays I'd written had been performed in various school and community theaters, and two more in regional. Those regional plays had been performed at The Marshall and had earned a more than respectable amount in ticket sales. But I'd be lying if I said my confidence hadn't been shaken after a stodgy old critic named Anderson Jones had slammed my two most recent plays. The revenue my scripts brought in was important, but the reputation gained by critical acclaim was what would keep me in the game. And get me on Broadway.

But those negative reviews had cracked the foundation of my Broadway dreams.

My only option to keep my career on track was to rally my nerves and write a killer script for the festival. No pressure.

I gave Babs a wide smile in thanks for the support. The kitchen door flew open and Noah Blake, the owner and Babs's stepson, appeared.

My back went up as my smile turned down.

With his lean, hard body that could only be gifted from God, dark hair, olive skin, and eyes the color of melted chocolate, Noah was often the subject of most women's fantasies here in Phair.

Girls might get their panties all wet at the sight of him, but I disagreed with the mainstream. My own private nickname for Noah was the Patron Saint of Assholes. His cold attitude to me made all that yummy maleness easy to look past. If he hadn't been my brother Quinn's college roommate at Columbia, we never would've met.

Too bad my brother hadn't gone to Stanford.

Too bad, also, that I'd taken a job in Phair the same time Noah was overseeing the opening of a new Double Shot bar. It meant I had to see him more than I would have liked. But with the Double Shot directly across from The Marshall Theater, where I both worked *and* lived, I found it tough to avoid him. There weren't a lot of other places in Phair where one could get a decent gin and tonic.

Noah strode through the bar, a crate of glasses on his shoulder. "Why the sour face all of a sudden, Training Wheels?"

I groaned at the hated nickname but refused to show him my irritation. He'd given it to me after I'd gotten drunk for the first time, sneaking mimosas during Quinn's college graduation brunch. After two glasses of

Moet-spiked OJ had caused me to throw up in a bowl of fruit salad, he'd deemed me forever in need of training wheels—unable to hold even the mildest of liquor.

While Quinn and Noah were in college, Noah and I had shared an affectionate relationship. Me being the little sister of his best friend and him being an only child with a tumultuous family life and therefore always at our house on college breaks, we'd bonded. But that was before he'd gone and ruined everything.

He passed me, then set the crate of glasses on the counter behind the bar.

"Since when does the majority shareholder of a multi-million dollar company empty the dishwasher?" I asked, adding a little snark to my tone, just to needle him.

"Since the bartender who was supposed to work tonight left town for a funeral." His gaze settled on my face. "The Double Shot is a family-owned enterprise, Wheels. No task is too menial."

Noah had climbed the ladder of his family's company since his father's death a while back. He'd taken the few bars his dad had founded around New York and turned them into a major chain, with locations throughout the US. Prior to coming to Phair seven months ago, I hadn't talked to him in three years—and only then because he'd come to my Grandma June's funeral in Dallas. Quinn had invited him for moral support, I supposed.

Babs cleared her throat and caught her stepson's attention. "Excuse me, *boss*, but speaking of menial tasks…" She jerked her thumb toward the other end of the bar. "Why don't you do us all a favor and fix the leaky pipe under the sink? Or are you too busy wheeling and dealing with investors?" When Noah ignored her, she shook her head and turned back to me, drumming her acrylic nails against the waist-high prep counter. Then she looked over my shoulder, past me, and straightened.

I followed her gaze. Lucas had arrived. Finally.

"Uh-oh," Babs said. "He isn't looking so good. What is it you Texans say?"

I filled in the blanks with my best native twang. "Looks like someone kicked his dog."

Dressed in a tweed jacket and bolo tie, Lucas also wore a defeated attitude that put a good ten years on the sixty-five he'd lived so far. I couldn't tell if his wrung-out appearance was because of the hundred-and-ten-degree late-August heat or if my earlier suspicions were true—something was majorly off.

Wearily sitting in the stool next to mine, he pulled out from an inside jacket pocket, the script I'd emailed earlier and set it on the bar in front of me. "I may have made a terrible mistake," he said.

A ball of dread formed and sat lodged somewhere beneath my windpipe. Babs, sensing tension, did the decent thing. She excused herself to check on three locals at the opposite end of the bar who were glued to a preseason Cowboys game playing on the oversized screen. Noah, however, stayed in place under the pretext of sliding glasses into an overhead rack, perfectly positioned to eavesdrop.

Though I hated the fact that I noticed, Noah's backside in those jeans drew my attention in a way I couldn't get past. He might be nosy and a pest, but damn it all, the local women were right—he was sexy as hell. Only right now, I didn't need the distraction.

"Should we grab a booth?" I asked Lucas.

"No need," he replied. "This will only take a minute."

Maybe I'd been overreacting earlier. If our conversation was supposed to only take a minute, the news couldn't be *that* bad. Could it? Plus, Lucas hadn't made a definitive statement. *I may have made a mistake* wasn't the same as *I made a mistake*. No sooner had the ball of dread sunk in my gut than it lurched back up to my throat. What if the dreaded reviewer Anderson Jones had signed on to be a judge in the upcoming festival?

"This…" Lucas said, gesturing at the script in front of me. "The Phair Theater Festival is four weeks away and this script still isn't finished."

With every word Lucas uttered, I shrank deeper and deeper into the back of my stool. I'd warned Lucas before I hit send this morning that the script for *Midnight in Summer* was not only unfinished, but also wasn't representative of my best work. My two main characters, Andy Rich and Caroline, weren't cooperating with me. But at the same time, I wasn't totally panicked about the script being incomplete. We were on target for the production for the Phair Theater Festival. Due to recycling from a previous show, the set was nearly complete, casting had been made, and the first act was close to perfection. With the actors already learning their lines to act 1, we were in good shape for when rehearsals officially began next week.

Evidently, Lucas saw things differently.

"I'm afraid, Ashlyn, I may have no choice but to look elsewhere for a script. You're so young, unseasoned. Too much is at stake to risk—"

"Whoa, whoa, whoa," Noah said, butting in.

If only I could get another three years of silence out of him… starting now. Damn him. I could handle this. I opened my mouth to protest, but he waved me off.

His gaze locked on Lucas. "Think this through. You're not the only one affected if The Marshall Theater Players production doesn't succeed at the festival."

What the hell was Noah talking about? And who did he think he was, interfering in my business? *Again.*

The ball of dread turned to a flare of anger. "This is a private conversation, Noah. Butt. Out." I turned back to Lucas. "Look, there are four weeks until the festival. Let me keep working on the script. I've pulled off bigger miracles in less time. I'm confident I'll do it again."

Lucas's normally kind eyes settled on me. "How well did the critics receive your last two plays?"

Now he was hitting below the belt, invoking the only critical flops in my small dossier. "You said yourself the theater made more money during the run of my plays than it has with any other playwright in ten years," I protested.

"That doesn't negate the fact that *critics* are the ones judging the contest."

"Aren't you the man who always says 'no two critics see the same show?' There are five judges, Lucas. As long as Anderson Jones isn't on the panel, we've got a good shot at taking top prize, even with an average script."

When Lucas raised his eyebrows at me, desperation took over, and I babbled on. "Regardless of the reviews and my age—or maybe because of it—people among the theater crowd are talking about me. About us."

"Ashlyn's right," Noah said, interrupting again. "You didn't bring her here to play it safe."

"No." Lucas reached for the Jack and Coke Noah set in front of him. "I brought her because of the brilliance she displayed in Arlington…which, I might add, *you* brought to my attention."

My gaze shifted from Lucas to Noah. I raised an eyebrow.

Arlington Community Theater had been on the brink of closure and needed a revitalization of public interest. My play *Little Lamb* had been edgy and controversial, but not so much that it deterred the humbling amounts of donations and ticket sales once word of it spread. It had been my only play under serious consideration of being published. But how did Noah know about any of that?

"Quinn told me you were on the brink of something special," Noah said, explaining the question he must've read in my arched look. "He wanted to see for himself, but couldn't leave Seattle at the time. I was curious and went."

My brother had talked about me to Noah? Told him about my being in Arlington? And Noah had gone—to see my play?

Wait... The dread that lined my gut gave way to bitterness as I realized the truth: the fact that I'd been hired by The Marshall Theater in the same town as the famed Double Shot had opened its most recent location was no coincidence, the way I'd thought.

How dare Noah help me land this job, especially after I'd been so clear with him years before that I didn't need his help? Or his interference.

I reached for my drink and drained half the contents, hoping the alcohol would miraculously calm my fury with Noah and allow me *not* to blow my shot at Broadway by saying something stupid in front of Lucas.

"The theater is facing bankruptcy, Ashlyn," Lucas said.

Bankruptcy? That got my attention.

Lucas nodded. "We make enough money in ticket sales and donations to pay our operational costs, but city inspectors are being forced to close us down due to building safety issues. Because the costs of repairs are so extensive, there is a very serious risk we'll have to close our doors for good."

The Marshall Theater had been in Lucas's family for well over a hundred years and was the heart and soul of the company. Without The Marshall Theater, there'd be no Marshall Theater Players.

Lucas went on. "This year marks the fiftieth anniversary of the annual Phair Theater Festival."

This much I knew.

"And this year, thanks to a special endowment, whatever theater company wins Best in Show will be awarded five million dollars."

My jaw unhinged.

The company who took top honors always received a substantial prize. Just like the top winning playwright and director always earned a short Broadway run—which was why I'd been so eager to take the job of writing this particular script for The Marshall Theater Players. I wanted a shot at seeing one of my plays produced on Broadway. But I had no idea the prize this year was so substantial for the theater company who won.

"With an award like that, The Marshall Theater could stay open," Lucas added.

The negative reviews from my last two plays filled my mind. Tension shoved away the shock. Maybe he was right. There was too much at stake. I was *way* out of my league.

Noah leaned in close to me. "Nine months ago, Lucas told me about the danger of theater closing. I knew there was only one person who could pull off the Hail Mary he needed. Your script could win The Marshall Theater Players that five million, and would keep the theater open."

I gulped. "Those stakes are high. What makes you so sure I can pull it off?"

"You already did it once."

Maybe. But could lightning strike twice?

"I also know about the contract," he added.

The contract?

He shot me a look and said quietly, "The one you signed with your father."

Heat suffused my face. God. Did Quinn have to tell him *everything*?

As executor of my grandmother's estate and on the night of my college graduation, my dad had offered to give me a one-time, fifty-thousand dollar distribution that allowed me to pursue my passion. In return, I had until my twenty-fifth birthday to prove I could make a substantive career as a playwright. If I failed, I would have to get a "real" job or else forfeit the remainder of my inheritance, which was one huge chunk of change. I'd only asked for one caveat: if I did end up failing, the remainder of my inheritance would go to a non-profit of my choice.

I'd been twenty-one at the time, fifty grand was a lot of money and four years had seemed like an eternity. Plenty of time to become a smashing success. So I'd signed the contract my father had drawn up. And had regretted the decision ever since.

Still, my dad had underestimated me and my dreams. He thought I'd take the cash, buy an expensive car, too many clothes and come crawling back home within six months. But I'd been thrifty. I even had some money left over. *Some* being the operative word.

"Quinn had no right to tell you any of that," I snapped out.

"You and I may not see eye to eye on much," Noah said, "but if there's one thing I can admire about you, it's your tenacity. When you're focused, you don't miss. You proved that with Arlington."

My gaze slid away from his. I didn't need to point out how untrue his latter statement was. I'd been focused on Noah once, had naively thought myself in love with him. Who knew falling in love could bring a playwright so much drama? I tried to mentally shove those memories back deep down, but the damage had been done.

Pain transitioned to anger. "I don't need you rushing to my aid," I said, heatedly. "Never have, never will. Besides, in case you've forgotten, I have a *real* brother, and guess what? I don't need him to take care of me, either."

"You think this is all about you?" Noah shook his head. His New York accent grew thick, the way it did when his temper reached its peak. "Are you so self-involved you *still* don't get it?"

I'd had enough. Standing, I slapped my palms on the bar and leaned toward Noah. "Maybe for once you could stop playing mind games and just tell me what the hell I'm *not* getting."

He gestured to the near-empty bar. "Look around. The theater's not in session, and because of that, this place is practically dead. What do you think will happen to the Double Shot if The Marshall Theater closes?"

"Why is it my job to care about the Double Shot?"

Noah had the audacity to look hurt. "Fine, I get it. You don't care about me, and maybe I deserve that, but what about the town? What about Phair?"

I looked around the bar. There were few patrons, certainly not enough to fill the place. Noah's words hit me—finally.

The Phair Theater Festival brought in boatloads of tourists, but only for one week of the year. The Marshall Theater Players, however, brought in tourists year-round, except for when the theater was dark. But the theater went dark only three times a year, for a four-week interval each time.

People raised families here, led lives, and made livings that were only possible because of tourism. The Marshall Theater was the lifeblood of Phair. Noah had multiple Double Shot bars scattered all over the country, but this location depended on Phair's local economy not falling into collapse.

And apparently, keeping the entire town of Phair alive depended on me writing a brilliant script.

Fantastic.

Lucas finished his drink, straightened his bolo, and stood. "It just occurred to me what's wrong with this draft."

I stared questioningly at Lucas.

"Noah is Andy Rich. You are Caroline."

I sat, perplexed. "What could possibly bring you to that conclusion?"

He nodded at both me and Noah. "Everyone can tell you two have history."

Neither Noah nor I had made any secret that my brother was his best friend. But what did that have to do with my script? "And your point would be…"

Lucas shrugged. "The tension between the two of you is palpable. Like the tension between Andy Rich and Caroline. You two *are* those characters."

No way. I took a step back, putting space between me and the bar. Between me and Noah. Lucas was dead wrong.

I pointed at Noah. "He is *not* the inspiration for my lead character." Not even Noah Blake was as damaged as Andy Rich. And I certainly wasn't the wannabe bad-girl, Caroline.

"I'm sure you subconsciously patterned the characters' dynamic around your dynamic with Noah," Lucas said. "But if you could manage to bring the same fire I've been witnessing between the two of you over the last few months to this play, we'll win Best in Show at the Phair Theater Festival. Even if Anderson Jones *is* a judge."

I was so not buying Lucas's observation. Yeah, Noah and I snapped at each other from time to time. Well, I snapped at him and he ignored me—*all* the time.

Lucas pulled out his wallet and laid cash for his drink on the bar. "Tell you what. I'll agree to stay the course and keep you on as playwright, but only if the two of you agree to work together."

Noah's chin lowered. "What exactly are you asking, Lucas?"

Yeah, really. What *was* Lucas asking?

"Spend time together. Help her flesh out what's missing on paper between these two characters."

"What?" Rattled, I raked fingers through my hair.

"That's insane," Noah said.

For once, Noah and I agreed on something.

"I'm not talking about just hanging out in the Double Shot, pretending to talk," Lucas said, rubbing his chin the way he did when new ideas came to him. "I'm talking scene enactment, and maybe some real-world situations. Improvisation."

But that would mean spending one-on-one time with Noah. Not just the occasional run-in at the Double Shot. I'd done my best to ignore Noah since I'd discovered his bar was my neighbor across-the-street, and could handle encountering him while I sat at the bar with a tumbler of gin in my hand, but this was too much. I felt pinpricks of panic work their way across my skin. "Lucas, no. Absolutely not."

"My decision is final, Ashlyn. Work on scene enactments and improvisation with Noah, or I'll assign another playwright to finish the script."

But this play was my chance at Broadway. It was also my chance to prove to my dad I could succeed in this business. I gulped back panic.

"There's no way I have time to play pretend with Ashlyn so she can finish her script," Noah said, scowling. "I have a business to build. I'm not playing babysitter."

Lucas turned to Noah. "According to you, the success of this Double Shot location depends on the success of the theater, which depends on The Marshal Theater Players winning the Phair Theater Festival. And you're the one who convinced me Ashlyn was a brilliant playwright in the first place. Looks like you don't have an option, either. You will both do this my way, or..."

"Or what?" Noah demanded.

I made a last-ditch plea. "Lucas, forcing us together will only hurt the situation, not help. Noah isn't even a writer."

A gleam entered Lucas's eyes. "He might not be a writer, but for this play, he's certainly your muse."

CHAPTER TWO

Noah

Through the large plate glass window, I watched Ashlyn—fine, I was checking out her ass—as she stormed out of the Double Shot and crossed the street, probably destined for her apartment on the top floor of the theater. The slump of her shoulders showed how the pressure of her situation held her down. When she slammed the theater door behind her, I folded my arms over my chest and frowned.

At the word "muse," Ashlyn had gone bat-shit crazy, huffing like a schoolgirl and storming out of the Double Shot. Lucas had followed, leaving me alone to figure out how to get myself out of this one. Why would Lucas say I was the inspiration for Ashlyn's lead character? Ashlyn had barely spoken to me since arriving in Phair. Well, except to snap at me.

So she needed to fix her script. I got that.

But Ashlyn and me hanging out, acting scenes from her play, was Lucas's way of solving the problem? That man might be a world-class director, but he was dead wrong in thinking me and Ashlyn in close proximity would solve anything.

But in one way, Lucas was right. Like it or not, we all had a stake in the outcome of the Festival.

And whether Ashlyn was writing for The Marshall Theater Players or a puppet theater, there still were only two more months until her birthday.

Quinn had shared the details of the deal she'd made with her dad. Prove herself as a playwright by the time she turned twenty-five, or lose her inheritance from her grandmother. And that was major money. This play was her last shot at the big time before then. Sue me for having faith in her. And screw me for wanting her to succeed. But I sure as hell didn't see how us being in close proximity would make that happen.

Besides. I didn't have time to pretend to be a character to trigger Ashlyn's muse. I had projects under my belt in need of my focus. Negotiations were under way regarding a partnership with a high-end hotel chain, the Cambridge Hotels, which was considering Phair for its next location. Then there was the international expansion I had planned. The Double Shot in London,

Paris, and Sydney. As it stood, I already didn't have enough hours in the day.

From the corner of my eye, I saw the wrench on the bottom shelf beneath the bar. I had a video conference in an hour, but a leaky sink was one thing I could fix. I grabbed the wrench and slid under the counter, ready to do battle with a recalcitrant pipe. But then the image of Ashlyn's tight ass as she stalked away consumed me. The very thought of being bound to her, even temporarily, did things to me I rather enjoyed thinking about—things her brother would disembowel me for if he ever knew. But he wouldn't know and neither would Ashlyn, because I'd never tell either. Quinn trusted me with his sister, and Ashlyn…well… Ashlyn hated me.

Sometimes the feeling was mutual.

But sometimes her presence brought with it a hard-on I had to hide.

Still didn't mean I would accept Lucas's ultimatum.

A few twists of the wrench, a bit of nasty water in my face, and the leaky pipe was repaired. I returned the wrench where I'd found it, wiped my face with my sleeve, and stood.

"Need some help, Noah?" asked one of the regulars. I'd nicknamed him Dusty because he worked for the road crew and came in, every night, covered in dust. He was tall, ham-fisted, and based on his burly build, hadn't missed any meals. Including the snack of the Double Shot's homemade potato chips that sat in front of him.

"Oh, now you offer," I grumbled. "*After* I'm done."

He grinned, then thumbed up the crumbs in his near-empty chip bowl. "Yell before you get started next time, wouldja?" His focus left me and returned to the game.

I cleared away his empty bowl and slid him a fresh one. Had we been in New York, Miami, or one of the ten other Double Shot locations, an offer like Dusty's wouldn't have been made. But that was how things worked around here—and why Phair had become my home in a way no city in the world ever could.

The front door opened. A smarmy-looking dude, wearing aviator sunglasses and dressed in pressed linen pants and a white button-up shirt, entered. Without acknowledgement, he bypassed the other patrons and approached the bar.

"I'll have a glass of red wine. French, if you have it," he demanded, an East Coast accent evident in his words. He took out a handkerchief and wiped nonexistent dust from the stool in front of him.

Wine? On a hot summer evening? The guy obviously wasn't from Texas. I nodded, and rummaged around in the drawer near the soda dispenser. "Are you a transplant?" I asked, referencing his accent. "Or here on vacation?"

He removed the sunglasses and placed them on the bar in front of him, then sat. "Business, actually. I'm a theater critic. I'm here for the festival."

After pulling the cork out of a fresh bottle, I poured the man's wine and set it in front of him, giving him a good once-over. Something about his disjointed nose and close-set eyes seemed vaguely familiar.

"You're a little early," I pointed out.

He smiled, slow and steady, revealing an even row of porcelain veneers. "You don't recognize me, do you, Blake?" I continued staring. Apparently not.

Before he finished, Babs was at my side. She'd piled a bowl high with potato chips, straight from the fryer, and set it on the bar for our new customer.

"Classy," he said, practically sneering at the chip bowl.

And right then that one word took me back—back to a seventeen-year-old Ashlyn, on the outs with her parents, running away to her brother's apartment in New York. Me going out to look for her when she didn't come home when she should have. Returning to the apartment, scared out of my mind when I couldn't locate her.

Hearing her voice, high-pitched and tense as I charged up the stairs to my apartment. Muffled speech. Sounds of a struggle. Then clearly, above everything else, the word *no*.

My fists clenched. Blood tunneled through my veins. In a snap, I reached across the bar, pulling Kyle Pritchard to me by his neck. Wine sloshed down the front of his white shirt as I pressed my thumb into his Adam's apple. "You've got a lot of nerve, you douchebag. Waltzing in here, sitting at *my* bar. If I so much as see you here, or even in the same room as Ashlyn, next time I won't just beat the shit out of you—I'll put you in the ground."

Pritchard's face grew red and he struggled to breathe. I relaxed my thumbs enough for him to speak.

In a rough voice, he said, "Staying away from Ashlyn might prove difficult, considering I'm a festival judge. And I know she's one of the playwrights."

I swore, but kept my grip. When he gave me a satisfied smirk, I wanted to pound his face in all over again. Then I heard Babs. "Noah," she said in a low tone. "Is this who I think it is?"

Two of the guys who'd been watching the game approached. Dusty and Haywire.

"You need some help, Noah?" Haywire, the city's electrical engineer, asked. Short and pole-thin, he looked like he couldn't shoo away a fly. But Haywire was a black belt in one of those weirdly named martial arts. The two men plus me would not equal a fair fight against Pritchard. Somehow I didn't care.

One of the wives, I couldn't see who, reached across the bar. Remote in hand, she flipped off the game mid-play. Not a single moan of protest was uttered by the men who'd been watching the game. The tension grew. All eyes remained on us.

Dusty inspected his nails. "So much for my manicure."

I opened my hand and shoved Kyle back by his throat. "He was just leaving."

Kyle staggered and swiped at the red wine staining his shirt. "You'll regret this, Blake."

As Dusty and Haywire saw our guest to the exit, Babs began clearing broken glass and spilled wine. Noise from the game once again filled the bar.

I hadn't been convinced Lucas's plan to be Ashlyn's constant companion was a sound one. Me, the owner of one of the fastest growing chain of bars in the nation, acting out scenes? Playing at improv? Yeah, right. But Kyle Pritchard's arrival in town had changed my mind. At the very least, Ashlyn needed someone watching her back.

It was only right that someone should be me.

The critic Anderson Jones and the chink he'd made in her confidence seemed like nothing compared to the damage Kyle Pritchard could inflict. I had to let her know he was in town and that he'd be judging her play. That was not a conversation I was looking forward to.

But Kyle's presence in the bar had brought out at least one positive. After the way Dusty and Haywire stood up with me, if I ever doubted my place in Phair, I did so no longer. Texans abided by a certain code when it came to right and wrong. And they *always* took care of their own. The way I'd take care of Ashlyn.

* * * *

The rest of the evening had been jam-packed with phone calls and video conferences with my attorneys. I hadn't gotten over to Ashlyn's yet to tell her about Pritchard. From my office across the street, I could see the light on in her apartment. I'd watched her silhouette cross the window as I set about taking care of what needed to be done.

I would follow Lucas's ultimatum just so I could protect her. But in doing so, I would need help keeping tabs on Kyle.

That's where Ashlyn's brother, Quinn, came in. If Ashlyn ever found out I'd betrayed her confidence and told her brother about what happened with Pritchard that summer, there'd be hell. But I'd gladly pay the price so long as it ensured her safety.

Quinn and I had been best friends since our undergrad days at Columbia. With his long, lanky build, paired with rust-colored hair and a short-sleeved plaid shirt, on first impression I thought he'd turn out to be a world-class dork. His techno-gadgetry genius only compounded that point. We called him Q in college, like the gadget guy in the Bond films. But he turned out to be pretty cool, and unbelievably got laid more than James Bond. He was also the only person I'd trust when it came to surveillance advice.

"Is this a bad time?" I asked when Quinn answered my request to video chat.

On the screen, I watched him finish off the last of a beer. The Seattle skyline featured prominently behind him—he had to be on his fifteenth floor balcony, enjoying the cool northwestern weather while I sweltered in Phair. "How's Vanessa?" I asked.

He settled back against light-colored cushions. "She dumped me four days ago. Said I work too much."

Quinn had used his share of his grandmother's legacy to patent and manufacture highly specialized surveillance equipment. That equipment had put his company, Q

Technologies, on the map. And kept his nose to the grindstone. Not much would get him to budge from Seattle.

"What's up in blistering Phair?" he asked. "That blazing sun's the one thing I don't miss about Texas."

"It's heating up, and I'm not talking about the weather." Guilt ran up my spine and into my gut. I'd kept Ashlyn's secret for years. But there was something about the way Pritchard had sneered, even when I had my hand around his throat, that made me figure he was up to something bad when it came to Ashlyn.

The smile fell from Quinn's face as I explained what had happened to her all those years ago. If he was pissed at me over it, he didn't let on. He simply leaned forward and listened as I pitched what I had in mind—a plan to keep close tabs on Pritchard.

Meanwhile, I kept flicking my gaze back and forth between Quinn on the computer screen and Ashlyn, across the street. She continued to pace in front of her windows.

Quinn finally agreed to my plan and I clicked off the conference call, then headed Ashlyn's way, intent on telling her Pritchard was in town. And intent on convincing her Lucas was right—we had to work together. I'd tell her that for the sake of her play, we had to go along with Lucas's ultimatum. What she wouldn't realize was that I'd be using Lucas's lame-brained idea to keep her safe from Pritchard.

To convince her I could do what Lucas suggested—pretend to be someone I wasn't—I'd brought along a prop, ready to show her just how dramatic I could be.

Moments later I stood at her door, one hand behind my back, hiding the prop I'd brought with me. I knocked once, waited. Twice.

The door opened. She stood, blinking at me. Then, without saying a word, she pulled ear buds from her ears and placed them, along with her iPod, on the table beside the door. Her arms dropped. "I don't have time for this, Noah."

Stepping through the threshold, I reached for her wrist and snapped on the cuffs, an abandoned favor from last week's bachelorette party at the Double Shot.

Her blue eyes widened, then she forced a controlled facade. She raised our conjoined wrists. "So you're into kink. But I don't think that's the way this is supposed to work. Obviously, you need pointers." She scanned the small, spartan room, consisting of a loveseat, coffee table, and a fake ficus tree. "I might have a fifty-shades-of-something book you could borrow."

With my cuffed hand, I reached behind me and closed the door, jerking Ashlyn's body against mine in the process.

Mistake.

My cock instantly hardened. All I could think about was how she smelled, like moonlight and summer. How her white tank clung to her torso, contoured over bare breasts to the point where I swore I could just make out the vaguest tinge of rose-colored nipples. How she turned me on without even trying, like no one ever had.

As my cuffed hand found hers and I finagled her arm so that it bent comfortably behind her back, wispy strands of auburn hair, twisted into an awkward bun at the side of her neck, tickled my face. Her pulse beneath my fingertips jumped. I inhaled her sweet scent as my heart rate went into overdrive along with hers. A primitive ache with the need to fill her settled in my bones.

But a man did not touch his best friend's little sister. Quinn had asked me years ago to look out for her, and as we'd pledged in our fraternity as freshman, a promise once made is never broken.

"The cuffs are to prove a point," I said. In spite of the warning going off in my head, my lips grazed her temple when my opposite arm circled her waist.

Ashlyn rose on toes, bringing us hip-to-hip so my erection was closer to where God intended, like she was testing how well we'd fit. Her eyes darkened a shade and I could tell she knew exactly what she was doing. Having her against me like this was bending the rules. Bending, I reminded myself, wasn't breaking. She also had that weird look—the one that told me she understood what I was thinking before I did.

It was also the look she got before she became the world's biggest smartass.

"So," she drawled out. "Not into kink. But it appears after all these years, I've been wrong about you. You're not a eunuch, after all."

"Not even close, sweetheart." My free hand covered her ass. My fingertips found bare skin beneath the curve of her shorts, and despite her bravado, she twitched.

About time she figured out who was in charge.

I continued. "If what Lucas said is true—that I'm the inspiration for your character—from now on, where I go, you go. Where you go, I go."

"Don't you think that's a little extreme? You do have a company to run."

"The point is I'm committed to seeing to it you get this script right."

Her eyes dropped to my lips. "You're saying you're willing to act out scenes with me?"

"Not exactly." I hadn't thought this part through well enough. "I'm no actor. But the improv stuff seems doable."

Ashlyn lowered herself to standing flat-footed and moved backward, attempting to create space between us. "That's too bad." The tip of her tongue darted out as she licked her lips. "There's one hot love scene between Andy and Caroline."

Damn her for fake flirting. Needing distance myself, I inserted the tiny key into the lock of the cuffs, setting us both free.

She rubbed her wrist and a frown wiped out the faux-seduction look she'd worn seconds ago. "What if I told you Lucas is right? He *should* find another writer, and another script."

"You don't mean that."

"What if I do?"

I stepped over a plate of barely eaten microwave pizza lying on the floor and took a spot on the slip-covered loveseat, discovering it had more lumps and craters than the surface of Mars. "Never figured you for a quitter, Wheels."

She picked up the plate. "No? Guess there's more to me than being self-involved."

Probably I deserved that. But having my words tossed back at me wasn't something I enjoyed.

I turned in my seat, watching Ashlyn as she took the plate to the kitchen and dropped it in the sink with a clatter. A bead of sweat ran along her temple. When she wiped it away, I realized the heat wasn't just the result of the friction between us.

"Jesus, it's like a sauna in here."

"You heard Lucas. The theater has no money. Even if the third floor AC wasn't blocked off, it's for performances only."

No wonder Wheels was having a hard time writing. Who could focus in this heat? She shouldn't keep living in a place with no AC. It was inhumane. An idea clicked. A way where I could use the pretext of us hanging out to follow Lucas's order *and* protect her all at once.

Mind made up, I stood. "Pack a bag. You're coming home with me."

Her eyes narrowed. "Excuse me?"

"Unless you like living in a sweat lodge, you'll be more comfortable at my house."

"Unbelievable," she said, walking around to stand in front of me. "You've got some nerve coming in here, ordering me around like I'm a child."

Ashlyn was right. I was acting like an authoritarian dick. At least my five-thousand square feet of living space would put some distance between us while still keeping her close.

"Lucas's mind is made up, Ashlyn. If you and I don't work together, we'll all lose. You, especially. That's one big fortune on the line. Your grandmother wanted you to have that money."

"I have two months until my twenty-fifth birthday. A lot can happen in sixty days—even without The Marshall Theater."

I held my hands up, a gesture of surrender, and figured I'd try acting contrite. "You're right, Wheels. I thought we'd be more comfortable at my place. Where there's air conditioning." I worked to soften my tone to contrition. "I'm sorry I acted demanding. I shouldn't treat people that way."

Something in her eyes softened and her shoulders slumped. For a minute, I actually thought she would give.

Then she said, "That's the thing. You *don't* treat people that way. For some reason, it's only me." She walked to the door and opened it. "It's late, Noah. Go home. But I'm staying here. I'm all out of fight tonight. I'll give Lucas my answer to his stupid plan in the morning."

Yeah, right. Like I was going anywhere.

I ignored the open door and kicked my feet up onto the coffee table. "You might as well grab me a pillow, Wheels. If you're staying, I'm staying."

Instead of slamming the door shut, Ashlyn gently closed it, secured the lock, and rubbed her eyes. "I wasn't kidding when I said I was all out of fight."

Ignoring my request for a pillow, she walked barefoot to her bedroom, and lay down under what apparently was the only fan in the apartment.

Leaving me alone, sweating in the heat.

CHAPTER THREE

Ashlyn

The mattress shifted. A hand came to rest on the curve of my spine. My own personal Adonis, in my bed. How lovely. I could feel the gentle rise and fall of his chest.

Wanting more, I moved closer. His hand slid to my hip. When fingers traveled down my leg, then back up, raised gooseflesh followed their path. Need ignited. Then he notched my leg over the outside of his thigh.

"I want you," I whispered.

God, I loved sex dreams.

Everything that made me a woman ached as he pressed his thickness against me in just the right spot. My hand traced the contours of his bicep, played over his muscled chest while his fingers continued their slow and glorious caress of my body.

And just as I reached for him to pull him closer, a flash of light brought me wide awake. The M on the shorted-out Marshall Theater sign had reclaimed life, and now the light filled the room.

Showing me I was *not* alone.

Oh, God. Not a dream.

Noah.

In my bed. Grinning at me in a most irritating way.

Mortified over what had almost happened—and worse, how much I'd wanted it to—I rolled to the edge of the bed and sat up. "What the hell do you think you're doing?" I demanded, pulling the sheet tight to my chest and kicking at him until he stood.

"I needed to borrow a toothbrush," he said, as if that explained everything.

"A toothbrush?"

He raked his fingers through his thick hair. "I came in to see if you had an extra toothbrush, but you were asleep. It's a million degrees in your living room. You have a fan. I figured I'd lie down for a minute. Get cooled off. I didn't mean to fall asleep. What happened wasn't supposed to happen."

His words, though true, were like an anvil on my heart, a fact that only served to irritate me more. "Of course it wasn't, because you weren't supposed to be in my bed."

"You know, you weren't entirely innocent in this, either."

"It's *my* bed, you jerk. I'm not the one who shouldn't have been in it."

"You're pissed because you liked it. Admit it, Wheels."

"I…just…argh." Witty comebacks were not my forte at four a.m. "Whatever you say, Noah." Exasperated, I stood and made a beeline for the bathroom. After a quick, cold shower to remove the sweat and any lingering trace of him from my skin, I threw open the bathroom door. Darkness and the ceiling fan chain *tinking* against the light bulb greeted me. The M had burned out again. Noah had taken off, but he'd left a note: *Need to work. Be back later. Think about what we should do for improv.*

I crumpled up the note and threw it across the room. Damn Noah and his assumptions. Just because he chose to kowtow to Lucas's crazy scheme didn't mean I would. There had to be another way to get the results we all needed.

Reaching for my laptop on the bedside table, I pulled up my current work in progress. What Lucas didn't know—rather, what I'd neglected to tell him—was that *Midnight in Summer* wasn't one of my typical scripts. I'd been working on it for years. It haunted me.

Why? Because Andy Rich's character moved me like no other. There was something about him, so tortured, so alpha, so… male, that compelled me like none ever had. And I had little doubt that if I could do him justice, he'd be a character remembered throughout the ages.

If only he hadn't met Caroline at the bus stop late that night. Her neediness had become the kryptonite to what could be a stellar script. But Andy was a guy who needed to be needed.

As I read through the pages again and again, a pattern emerged. Lucas had a point. A very, very small one. There were definitely similarities between Noah and Andy in their need to piss on their territory and take charge. But Andy also had a soft side, one that Noah lacked.

Noah believed there wasn't a problem that couldn't be solved. Sometimes even with a fist. His past proved that.

While I respected Lucas's opinion and his instincts, he was dead wrong here. Noah Blake was certainly not my muse.

And I most assuredly wasn't the virgin-turned-temptress Caroline.

* * * *

After a few hours of wrestling with the script, I made coffee, had a yogurt, then decided I was getting nowhere. Lucas's plan and Noah's lame response had me focused on my own irritation and not Caroline's motivation. Lucas was wrong—having Noah around was the last thing I needed to inspire my writing.

I left my apartment and wound my way through the interior of the theater, hoping to catch my good friend, Jessica Jackson, down in the costume workroom. If anyone could help me sort through details and gain some perspective, it would be her. But as I tromped down the musty stairwell, I couldn't keep my mind from shifting to last night.

Damn Lucas and his ridiculous ultimatum. He honestly believed that forcing Noah and me to work together was the only way to wrangle a great script from me. I just needed to prove to him that writing plays and skinning cats were one and the same— there was more than one way. And that way didn't involve getting deliciously felt up in the dark by the Patron Saint of Assholes.

"I need a favor," I said, finding Jessica sitting in the workroom on the first floor, exactly where I expected she'd be.

"Well, good"—she turned a slim wrist and checked her watch—"afternoon to you, too."

"I'm sorry." I gave her a quick grin, knowing she'd forgive my rudeness. Then I got sidetracked by the hundreds of beads covering the table in front of her. A second later, she pulled up a cape that'd covered her lap. "Is that Caroline's?" I asked.

"As a matter of fact, it is." Jess handed the cape over to me, then used a knitting needle to secure her long, honey-colored hair into a bun on top of her head. Her green eyes sparkled as I salivated over the cape, admiring what had been hours of work.

As costume designer for the theater, Jessica also worked with the local dry cleaner, doing alterations on the side. Besides supplementing her income, it was an added perk that they allowed her to take home unclaimed merchandise. What she didn't use for the theater she remade to sell online. But this wasn't for profit. This cape was pure Caroline.

"In that first scene, with the San Francisco fog rolling through and Caroline dressed in her formal best…this is absolutely perfect." Then I checked the label. "It's designer. You'll get hundreds, maybe even a thousand dollars on resale."

"More than that if we take Best in Show at the festival and this baby follows you to Broadway."

"And that leads me to why I'm here." I handed the cape back over to Jess and explained Lucas's crazy idea. How Noah had finagled it so that Lucas brought me to Phair when he found out the theater was in trouble. How Lucas now believed getting past my block hinged on teaming up with Noah. How Noah later showed up at my place with handcuffs and a point to prove.

And worst of all, how his late-night visit to my bed had not only rattled my nerves, but also became the cause of an intense script review that cracked through my denial and made me seriously consider whether Lucas might actually be right.

Through it all, Jessica listened, nodded occasionally, and saved her comments for the end.

"The success of your script would be huge. Lucas had a meeting with city officials yesterday," Jess said, "trying to buy us more time after the festival. They wouldn't budge."

"You knew about this and didn't tell me?"

"Rumors have been circulating for a while now."

Of course they had. You could expect nothing less in a small town.

"Lucas will break it to the cast the first night of rehearsals." Jess stood. Using a fabric ruler, she swiped beads into a plastic storage container the size of a large shoe box. "I'll be honest with you though, when I spoke to Lucas, he seemed excited about the script."

Had Lucas been playing mind tricks, assuming I'd rise under pressure? Or had Jessica talked to him before his read-through?

I bent to pick up the beads that had fallen to the floor. "What exactly did he say?"

"That *Midnight in Summer* has stellar potential."

Potential. Right.

I put the dropped beads in the container Jess held and she sealed the lid. Then I pulled the rolled-up script from the back pocket of my shorts and handed it over. Having grown up in the theater with actors for parents, Jess had developed perceptions different from most. Because of that, I figured I could trust her judgment.

"Will you read it?" I asked. "I need an objective opinion. Is Noah Andy Rich? Am I Caroline? You're the only person who knows I once had a crush on Noah."

"Look, Ash. I'd love to read this and give you a different perspective, but I don't know Noah like you do. And neither does Lucas."

I glanced down at my hands, realizing I'd been giving them a melodramatic wring, then looked back up at Jess.

Noticing my hands, Jessica's eyes narrowed. "This theory Lucas has and his plan to get you back on track—what is it *really* about his idea that has you so worked up?"

A bead of cold sweat ran down the center of my back. "I'm not following."

"What is it you're so afraid of, Ash? Personal failure? Letting your father win and lose your inheritance? Or that you'll actually like spending time with Noah?"

Her observation was way off-base and totally unfounded. She knew how I despised Noah and his constant interference in my life. Jessica's comment made me second-guess her objectivity. "The Marshall Theater is special, Jess. It's the lifeblood of Phair. And as much as I dislike the idea of letting my father win without putting up one last fight, I also couldn't bear it if the fate of an entire town was hitched to my falling star."

"You're not understanding what I meant."

I huffed. "So maybe speak in plain English."

She gave me one of those looks only a friend can give, took a deep breath, then exhaled and spoke slowly. "What I meant is, are you afraid you might fall in love with Noah Blake all over again?"

CHAPTER FOUR

Noah

Damn plumbing. No sooner had I fixed one leak than another started—one much more serious than the last. Luckily Babs had been in the cellar, bringing up extra bottles of wine, when the pressure valve burst. She'd interrupted me in the middle of an important business call because no one in the bar knew where the main shut-off to the line was. Guess that's what I got for not telling Ashlyn that Kyle Pritchard was in town. *And* that he was a festival judge. Karmic retribution.

I'd headed over to Ashlyn's the night before, intent on getting her to agree to Lucas's plan so I could implement a secret one of my own: protect Ashlyn from dickhead Pritchard. But she'd sulked off to bed before I could even work up to the topic. Since I'd had a video conference with my London expansion team at 4:00 a.m., I'd taken off after she'd stormed into the bathroom, pissed at finding me in her bed. And probably more pissed because she'd liked it.

But I hadn't left her unprotected. From both my office and the bar, I had a straight shot at the side door of the theater that led to her apartment. Pritchard hadn't shown up all day.

Plumbing issues squared away with the professionals now fixing the problem, I sat back down behind the desk of my upstairs office and picked up the phone. Before I could make a call, Babs came through the door.

"Plumbers found an old AC unit in the cellar," she said. "Want me to have them recycle it?"

"Sure." I leaned back in my chair, giving her a look. "I got an e-mail from the CEO of Cambridge Hotels."

Her brows rose. "Oh?"

"They got the specs I had forwarded. They're interested in partnering with the Double Shot, and they think Phair is the perfect location for their new resort. Told you they'd bite."

"Cambridge is swanky. A partnership with the Double Shot will generate additional tourists. Will that solve the threat losing the theater has on Phair?" she asked.

"If the deal goes through, it won't save the theater, but it will go a long way toward helping the town."

Babs pulled her e-cig from the front pocket of her skirt, lit up, then said, "Better watch it, son. If word gets out you had anything to do with this, you might get yourself elected mayor on a write-in ballot." She took a final drag on her fake cigarette and headed toward the door. "Soon as the plumbers are done, I'll have 'em haul away that air conditioner."

"Wait," I said. I'd been so wrapped up in my own dealings I'd forgotten something. "Are we talking part of an HVAC system, or the kind that goes in the window?"

Babs shrugged. "I didn't see it."

I stood. "I'll go check it out."

As it turned out, what sat in the basement was an old window unit air conditioner that worked like a dream. Since Ashlyn refused my offer to stay at my place, I figured she could use it to cool down that furnace she called an apartment. I'd made a plan to stick by her side, making sure she accepted and followed through with Lucas's scheme, no matter if the plan was outrageous. And I didn't want to sweat myself to death doing it.

Even as I strapped the unit to a dolly, I knew my justification was partly a ruse. Remembering the way she'd fit against me in her bed turned me on again. I could still hear the breathiness of her whisper echoing in my ears. *I want you.*

Jesus, this line of thinking had to stop. The fastest way to lose a friend was to go after said friend's baby sister, and I didn't want to lose Quinn as a friend.

But even if I went after her, what of substance could I offer her—or any woman, for that matter? There was something toxic in my system. Something given to me by my father. Some inheritances are good—and some are dangerous.

Ashlyn had gotten a glimpse of that bad side when I'd found her alone in my apartment with Pritchard. It was no wonder she held a grudge against me. Why she despised me.

If only I hadn't left her that day.

Nothing I could do to rectify the past, though. Shaking myself from my funk, I shoved the AC, strapped to the dolly, through the main area of the bar and called out to Babs, "Heading out for a while."

She hollered back, saying, "How did Ashlyn take hearing Kyle Pritchard is in town?"

It had been out of necessity to keep Ashlyn safe that I'd broken my promise and told Quinn about what had happened between Ashlyn and Pritchard. Babs, on the other hand, had known all along. Babs had been to Ashlyn what she didn't have—a mother figure to guide her—and what I couldn't be—a shoulder to lean on.

"Last night wasn't a good time," I said. Just as I was about to shove open the main doors, I caught a glimpse through the front window. Pritchard had rounded the corner, moving in the opposite direction of the theater, thank god. At least I didn't have to go chase him away from Ashlyn.

In pressed khakis and a white shirt, he looked like he should've been headed for lunch at the yacht club rather than wandering the streets of Phair. From the looks of it though, those pants were about to get dirty. Because of my angle inside the bar, I could see what he couldn't— the mayor's youngest kid hauling ass down the sidewalk on his skateboard along the cross street.

Pritchard noticed the kid and back-stepped, missing the boy by no more than a hairsbreadth, then his arm shot out and he caught the kid by the back of his shirt, wrenching him out of the way a split second before a silver minivan accelerated through a red light. Pritchard catapulted himself to brace the boy's fall with his body, and the van sped on, crushing the skateboard beneath spinning tires.

Holy shit.

Pedestrians and street vendors looked on, mouths open like big-mouthed bass, before rushing to give aid. Another bystander stepped from behind a car, pulled out a cell phone, and snapped photos.

"Did Pritchard just do what I think he did?" Babs asked, coming up beside me.

"Yup."

"He saved that boy's life. Huh." Babs stood silent for a moment, then asked, "Any chance the leopard changed his spots?"

I shrugged, then stared at the crowd of people making a fuss over Pritchard, fawning all over him like he was some sort of hero. Hero, my ass.

Leopards don't change anything. Once a predator, always a predator, in my mind.

* * * *

Pulling sixty pounds up three flights of stairs to Ashlyn's apartment was no easy feat when the path from point A to B was hotter than the Sahara in mid-summer. Thankfully, this time she answered on the first knock.

Instead of inviting me in, she leaned her hip against the door jamb and crossed her arms. "If it isn't the Patron Saint of Assholes."

Damn she looked good, even with no make-up and her hair pulled up in some kind of funky twist. The light sprinkling of freckles across the bridge of her nose added the perfect amount of character. And that smart mouth of hers with those full and red lips—instinct told me if I ever planned to get past its bitterness, it'd be the gateway drug to her essence.

My glance slid lower. This time she was wearing a bra. I didn't know whether to be relieved or disappointed. Either way, it was a fight to move my eyes back up on hers.

"Stop staring at my breasts," she said.

As if it were that simple. "Put the claws away. I came with a peace offering."

"You think that's going to make up for dry humping me in my sleep?"

She was being dramatic. There'd been no humping. "What? A free AC isn't good enough? You holding out for five carats and a marriage proposal to restore your good name?"

"Wonder what Quinn would say if I called him up and told him how you attempted to steal my virtue?"

Now that got to me. I hadn't been the only one last night feeling a certain something. "The way you wrapped yourself around me, Wheels, and how I distinctly remember you carrying on and on about how much you wanted me, makes me think your perception of my actions is a bit off."

Her nostrils flared. She knew I had her. "You're lucky I'm in a forgiving mood today, Noah. At the moment, I'd take cold air over anything...except maybe an emerald cut, six-carat canary. I have higher standards than five." Laughter lit her baby-blues.

Should've known she was trying to goad me. "Look, I didn't come here to word-spar. Do you want the AC or not?"

"Depends. What's it going to cost me?"

That was a loaded question. "Have you considered Lucas's deal?"

"What if I say I'm weighing my options? Will you let me have the AC anyway?"

"Are you at least weighing them with an open mind?"

A slight smile turned up her lips and she stepped out of the way. Something I took to be a good sign.

After pulling the dolly through the door, I raised the bottom of my shirt and wiped sweat from my upper lip. When I looked back at Ashlyn, her gaze had dropped to my bare stomach, the shade of her eyes teetering on midnight. "Now who's staring, Wheels?"

For a split second I would've swore her cheeks flushed.

"What?" Her face returned to the picture of innocence. "You have a sexy stomach. I mean, it's not all ripped like a *Men's Health* model, but it's not bad, either."

Knocked off-balance by the compliment, albeit a backhanded one, I rubbed my neck, trying to collect myself and calm the growing situation in my pants.

"What's the matter, Noah? Can't handle it when the shoe's on the other foot?"

"What do you mean?"

"You can stare at my breasts, but I can't return the gesture?"

"My breasts aren't nearly as attractive as yours."

"Which is why I was forced to look lower." She flashed that big-toothed grin that made a man want to bend to her will. Or just bend her over.

Jesus, she was killing me.

I cleared my throat. "You know, a gracious hostess would offer her guest something to drink."

"You're right," she said, still smiling. "Forgive me."

I wanted to wipe that smirk off her lips. Or kiss it off. Instead, after following her into her apartment, I quietly waited for her to get a water bottle out of the fridge. I took the cold drink she offered and ignored the extra charge I got at the center of my gut when our fingers brushed in the exchange. I drained the water in three gulps, then nodded to the AC unit. "Want me to hook this thing up or not?"

She replaced the lid and set the empty bottle aside. Then she licked her lips. "How about we try the bedroom?"

Shock sparred with confusion. "Excuse me?"

"The windows in here are too wide and they face the street. There's a window in the bedroom that's smaller and faces the alley. Structurally, the casement there would be a better fit."

I cocked my head and almost grinned. "You seem sure of yourself."

"Irrespective of popular belief, not *all* women have poor spatial perception. I'm a great judge at seeing how seemingly large objects can fit into tight spaces."

Intentional or not, her sexual innuendo hit its mark right below my belt. After a couple of deep breaths and a quick visualization of New York City streets on trash day, I somehow managed to get the situation back under control.

I followed Ashlyn into her bedroom, which in daylight appeared more spacious than the living room-kitchen combo, only not by much. Maybe that was because the living room was as neat as my old man's tumbler of whiskey. The bedroom, however, looked more like what'd happened after one of his benders—something I hadn't noticed in last night's darkness.

What I guessed to be dirty clothes were strewn about the floor and on top of an army-style trunk. Laundry day had come and gone over the last few weeks, it seemed. Books and magazines made mounds like gopher holes. A nightstand, littered with water bottles and a lone lamp, stood to the side.

Good God, Ashlyn was a slob.

My gaze went to the bed, topped by a tangled mess of sheets. My mind instantly returned to last night. So did the rest of my body.

Using the AC to block what was certain to become visible discomfort, I unstrapped the unit and carried it the short distance to the window. Ashlyn followed me, but I kept my back to her until things settled down, giving my body a silent lecture on how its reaction to her was becoming an irritating habit.

With Ashlyn's help, installing the AC unit took no time. Within minutes, cold air flowed from the vents. Ashlyn stood in front of the window, eyes closed, arms and legs spread. On her face she wore an expression of ecstasy. When she turned and raised the tail of her shirt to let the air play over her back, I caught enough of a glimpse of her midriff to make me wish it was my hands on her skin.

Seconds later her gaze locked with mine. In a move I didn't see coming, she stepped forward. Her arms looped around my neck. What the hell?

CHAPTER FIVE

Ashlyn

"Thank you, Noah," I said, instinctively pulling him to me in a hug. Installing the AC had been a sweet gesture, reminding me that occasionally Noah's massive savior complex paid dividends. The heat had sweltered my resistance to his control, and I couldn't summon up enough bitch to be anything except grateful.

At first his body stiffened, but then his arms circled my waist, pulling me so close I could feel the uneven beat of his heart pounding as we met, chest to chest. Damn he felt good, all hard muscles and the heady scent of man.

Slowly, I pulled back but not away, looked into his dark chocolate eyes, fighting against a force inside myself that was as natural as it was unwelcoming. Noah and I had been here before. He'd walked away and I'd faced a devastation so great it caused me to make stupid choices—ones that left me weak and distrusting of men.

Ones that left me feeling no better than my character, Caroline.

The past was done and I couldn't change it. But what if Caroline's story could be different? What would happen if Caroline decided to make different decisions? To go for what she wanted rather than running from what she feared?

My gaze traveled to his lips, full and determined. His face, however, wore an expression of puzzlement. Like he couldn't figure out why I'd hugged him. Or why I wasn't stepping back.

I couldn't figure it out, either.

But the more I thought about it, the more I realized Lucas was right. Well, kind-of right. Noah wasn't Andy Rich, but that single hug had me rethinking Caroline.

The night Caroline and Andy met, they'd kissed. One fateful meeting had changed their lives forever. One kiss had bonded them for good.

Or bad.

Depending on how you looked at it.

So what would it feel like for Caroline to kiss Andy Rich? I know how much I'd wanted to kiss Noah all those years ago. And now, with him so close, smelling like hot, sweaty male, having done something just like what Andy would have done for Caroline, I felt those long-suppressed stirrings.

What would kissing Andy Rich for the first time be like for Caroline?

One of Noah's hands roamed, reeling me in as his palm held the small of my back firm, tightening his hold on me and bringing our hips into contact. The world swirled around me and I leaned into him. Slid my hand up to fit around the back of his neck.

My fingers entwined in his hair and I raised my mouth to meet his.

The kiss that followed was slow and soft, not at all what I expected from someone usually wound so tight. He filled my senses, just the same. Noah's lips were firm, yet giving. His mouth hot, but it didn't burn. Ripples of pleasure rolled through me as our lips melded. Tongues played an unhurried game of seek and find.

He deepened the kiss and I got swept away. Only it was more than his mastery over the physical act that drew me in and held me under. It was riding the wave of rightness. Feeling like I'd found a place I belonged.

And my God, did I want him, with every pulse of my quickened heart.

His hand found its way under my shirt. Fingers drifted over bare skin, leaving nothing but an intense need for Noah in its wake.

Wait.

No.

Not Noah…Andy. This was about Caroline and Andy.

Oh, hell.

I wrenched my lips away from his. Noah dropped his arms from around me and stepped back. My eyes opened wide just as his were beginning to clear.

For a minute there, my signals had gotten crossed. It was a mistake I wouldn't make in the future.

The future…

Surprised at my own revelation, I allowed the weight of acceptance to sink in. I would jump in with both feet and follow Lucas's hare-brained idea, but only because I'd tried everything else to finish this play, to no avail. And for me, it wasn't just a theater or a bar or money at stake. It was Broadway. And what did Broadway represent? The ability to make it in this world on my terms. I'd prove to my father I could be successful *my* way.

God, now I was being overdramatic. Even so, I was ready to cue Sinatra and get on with the show.

I could only imagine Jessica's smug look of satisfaction when I admitted to her she'd been right. I *had* been afraid of falling for Noah again. But as long as I kept my heart guarded and my back up, there wasn't a chance of that. I would play the part of Caroline in the hope of understanding her better, and to crawl inside the mind of Andy Rich.

Finally, looking into Noah's eyes and for the first time really seeing, I grinned. "So this is it. This is what it feels like to kiss Andy Rich."

His eyes darkened and his body went stiff. "Does this mean you're on board with Lucas's plan?"

"Yeah." The tips of my fingers played over my lower lip, still warm from the heat of his kiss. "I think it does. Isn't that the reason you came?"

Something in the flash of his eyes and tenseness of his jaw revealed the fact that his smile seemed forced rather than genuine. "I have work that needs my attention. We'll finish this conversation later."

* * * *

The slamming of my front door signaled Noah's departure and gave a clear indication he wasn't happy.

But why?

He'd gotten what he came for. I'd given him my alliance in an attempt to save the theater and the town.

This *was* all about Andy and Caroline, right?

I sank down on my bed, letting the cool air blow over me. It all felt so surreal. Had I *really* kissed Noah? The taste of him—that intoxicating blend of spices that was hard-core Noah—had imprinted itself on my tongue. And what was even more surprising than the fact I'd actually kissed him was how good it had felt.

Like, *amazingly* good.

But it was never going to happen between us. Not in any *real* sense, at least. This was about the play and only the play. Besides, I'd almost offered myself to him once—body, mind, and soul— and what had he done? He'd thrown it back in my face, leaving me to fend for myself.

With a spine of steel, I pulled myself together, got off the bed, and traveled the short distance to the living room and my computer.

Now that the temperature in the apartment was becoming notably cooler, maybe I could focus. Long since used to the off-kilter lumps of the loveseat, I plopped down and opened my laptop. As I began rereading old thoughts and cataloging new, I realized things had changed. Maybe even dramatically. I could *feel* Andy now…smell him…taste him. By the time I finished making a few small changes to act 1, a knock sounded at my door.

The moment I cranked the lock back, Jessica barreled through, dressed in combat boots, short camo shorts with matching tank top, and pigtails. For a second I stood, staring in awe at her. With girl-next-door good looks, Jess effortlessly pulled off outfits that would've made the rest of us appear attention-hungry.

The moment I closed the door, she rubbed her arms. "Brrr. Am I coming down with something, or is it cold in here?"

"Noah," I said with a half-bitter smile. "Coming to my rescue. Again."

"Wish I had a hot guy swooping in to save me now and then."

Jess knew about my past with Noah. Actually, she knew Noah and I had known each other for years, and that he and I didn't exactly get along. I'd never told her why. I'd shared with her my once-upon-a-time crush I'd had on him and how we'd almost kissed, but hadn't gone into detail about what had followed.

Jess cocked her head. "Ever think maybe Noah wanted you in Phair for something more than to save the theater?"

The reminder of how I'd come to get my job at The Marshall Theater rubbed me raw. "You mean something other than feeding his God complex?" While I was happy at the opportunity to come to Phair, it was one I'd wanted to earn by my own merit, not by Noah stepping in and pulling strings. I still couldn't get over the fact that he'd been the one to point Lucas in my direction.

Jess followed as I returned to my spot on the loveseat. She sat beside me. "Seems to me there's a lot of unfinished business between you two. If you decide to work together, do you think you can finagle around all this pent-up anger you have toward him?"

I let out an audible breath and rolled my head to loosen the muscles in my neck. "I hope we can. I mean, Noah's already said there's no way in hell he's going to act out any of the *Midnight in Summer* scenes. Thing is, without him even knowing it, we kinda just did."

Her brows rose and she sucked in her cheeks. "Do tell."

"It was an experiment." I nibbled my lower lip. "I kissed him."

Just because I'd been channeling Caroline, kissing anyone like that was totally out of character for me. Now that my actions had sunk in, I felt a strange sort of liberation. For once, I was completely in control.

"But you've kissed Noah before, right?" Jess asked.

"Almost. He stopped himself just before it happened." I pulled at a loose thread on the arm of the loveseat. "Funny, but that was the same day I met Kyle Pritchard," I murmured.

"Who?"

Too late, I realize I'd said that out loud. "A jerk. Never mind." Tucking her leg beneath her, Jess angled her body toward me. "I read your script, Ash. Seems like there's a hint of your past there. What happened between you and Noah? And what does this Kyle Pritchard guy have to do with it?"

"Argh." I scrubbed my hands over my face. "What happened was how I became a poster child for the young and stupid."

"All teenagers are idiots."

"Me more so."

"Ashlyn, tell me." Her voice was firm.

I sighed. I could pretend like nothing had happened, or tell the truth. I went with truth. Jessica deserved to know, because hers was one of the many futures caught in the crossfire. "I was seventeen. Summer between my junior and senior years. I fought with my parents and ran away, taking the train to New York. I'd planned to stay with my brother. But I had my weeks off and missed Quinn by a day—he'd already taken off for a backpacking trip in Europe. But Noah was there, staying in the apartment. He called my parents and told them I was safe. He even convinced them I should stay there until things blew over. Said he'd watch over me while I cooled off."

I smiled, remembering the fun we'd had. Noah taught me how to use the subway, took me to museums, concerts in Central Park, and even got us backstage passes to a few Broadway shows.

"What were you fighting with your parents over?"

"College. I was never the all-star student like Quinn. When I said he's a genius, I meant it literally. Visiting him when he was at Columbia was how I fell in love with New York. I had my sights set on NYU. My father wanted SMU because it was his alma mater and close to home."

"Where he could keep you under his thumb, right?"

I gave Jess a little smile. "Exactly."

She twisted a strand of hair around her finger and met my gaze. "So, basically you were running away from your family because of the life your father was choosing for you."

An itchy feeling in that hard-to-reach place in the center of my back settled. "You could say that."

"Sort of like how twenty-year-old Caroline ditched her own engagement party in 1957."

I opened my mouth and closed it. When she put it like that, certain similarities between Caroline and me became obvious.

"Oh, God," Jess said, recognition dawning on her face. "If your story is Caroline's story," she continued slowly, "then you must have met some young, wealthy guy at a play, Andy Rich—well, *Noah*—had invited you to but then bailed on going. You tell the handsome stranger you're an aspiring playwright. He feeds you a line about getting your script in front of his famous producer father."

I shot her a look that said she was dead on, then swallowed the sour taste in my mouth. I hated reliving this part of my past. Maybe that's why the play had remained stuck in Neutral for so long. "Yep. His name was Kyle Pritchard. And like Caroline, I naively invited him back to Noah and Quinn's apartment with the intention of giving him said script."

Jess's expression changed, anger pinching her eyebrows together. "Kyle takes that as his right to force his way into your pants."

I wrapped it up by adding, "Except Noah showed up, sans superhero cape, to save the day."

For a moment, Jess sat silent, staring at the floor. Finally, she looked up at me. "Did Noah, uh, show up in time?"

"I was handling it. I could have handled it. But instead…" I bit my lip, cutting off my words, unwilling to bring the images that had followed to mind. "I've never asked for Noah's help. Not then, not now."

"Doesn't matter. Maybe it's the fact that you're his best friend's sister, but my guess is it's guilt. He feels responsible for you."

"Never mind. I wanted your objective opinion on the script,"

I said, shaking my head. "I guess I have my answer."

"You are Caroline and Noah is Andy."

I sunk deeper into a lump in the loveseat. "So how do I fix it?"

"Fix what?" she said, grinning. "The script, or what's between you and Noah?"

I shot her a baleful look.

Jess pulled her leg out from underneath her, mimicking my position on the loveseat. "Hell if I know."

By the time Jessica left, I was exhausted beyond belief. I laid my head against the arm of the loveseat and closed my eyes, trying not to let situations overwhelm me. The sound of a car horn going off kept me from being lulled to sleep by the rhythmic hum of the AC. Before calm could return, another knock sounded. Figuring it was Jess, I called out, "Come in."

Only it wasn't Jess who waltzed through my door. Instead, Noah entered, carrying the largest and probably oldest beanbag I'd ever seen with one hand, a six-pack of beer with the other.

"What the hell?" I eyed the lumpy corduroy-covered cushion in disgust.

"In case you haven't noticed, Wheels, you're a little sparse on furniture."

"I've been living in Phair for seven months. It's too late for a housewarming, don't you think?"

"Nope," he said. "Trust me. This is exactly what you need. It's seen me through many hard times and tough decisions. In fact, I'm not positive I didn't lose my virginity on this thing."

"That's disgusting."

His eyes softened, along with his tone. "My mother bought it for me when I was seven."

In all the years I'd known him, I'd never heard Noah even mention his mother. Not that we were close and shared those intimate details about our lives the way girls do. But there'd been a time when we were friends. Still, I'd never asked him about why his mom had taken off, or why he had such a bad relationship with his father. But I had my suspicions.

Tossing the beanbag into an empty corner, he took the beer to the fridge. When he came back, he said, "Come on, Wheels, give it a try."

"I'm not sitting on that thing after you've desecrated it." In spite of my protests, he pulled me from the loveseat. "Relax. The cover is removable. It's been decontaminated many times over." With a gentle nudge, he propelled me onto the beanbag.

Engulfed in a cocoon of softness, I wiggled until I worked myself into a perfect position.

"Now, just imagine your computer right here," he said, motioning to the space across my legs. "Your neck is fully supported and all the pressure's off your limbs. Isn't it much better than that old allergen-infested lump of dust?" He cocked his head toward the loveseat.

"There's nothing wrong with that lump of dust. I *did* actually clean it after I dragged it out of the dumpster. It took an entire bottle of Febreze."

"You just made my point." His smile lit his entire face. The effect left me breathless.

Tears pricked my eyes at his sudden show of kindness, which was in direct contrast with how we'd left things before.

"What's this?" He kneeled in front of me and wiped the wetness away with the pad of his thumb. In the same motion, he tucked a loose strand of hair behind my ears. "Why are you crying, sweetheart?"

"I'm just tired, I guess. I didn't get much sleep last night."

He had the decency to look guilty.

"And you're stressed."

I took a shaky breath. "Why are you being so nice?"

"How about we agree to take a break from all the head-butting?"

Closing my eyes, I pinched the bridge of my nose, trying to stave off a downpour.

With the back of his fingers, Noah reached out and stroked my cheek. "Maybe if we lay down our swords and work together for a couple of weeks, we'll figure a way out of this mess." He held out his hand. "What do you say? Truce?"

I nodded and slipped my hand into the cradle of his, allowing its warmth to envelop me. "Truce."

"We can all win, here. I want that more than anything, especially for you."

"Why?" My gaze settled on the fine lines at the corner of his eyes—proof of frequent smiles and a certain charm the college-aged version of Noah had lacked. "Why is it so important to you that *I especially* succeed?"

"Because the sooner you get your shot on Broadway, the sooner you're out of my hair for good." His lips twitched at the corners.

I couldn't help myself. I had to laugh at his comeback, knowing I'd totally set myself up for it. But the moment I did, other emotions took over and the floodgate of tears opened.

"Damn," Noah said. "I hate it when I make girls cry." He positioned himself next to me on the bag more than big enough to accommodate us both. Arms wrapped tight around me, he kissed my temple. "I promise, sweetheart. It's going to be okay."

If only I could believe it was true.

Chapter Six

Noah

This was crazy.

Absolutely nuts.

Part of me couldn't help thinking Ashlyn was wielding her power over our truce, all in an attempt to see how far she could push me. I told her I'd rather rot than do anything remotely resembling scene enactment, but the day after our agreement to follow Lucas's plan, Ashlyn had a new idea, one she'd been so excited about even I couldn't deny her.

In this scene, Andy was supposed to be stalking Caroline. Why? I had no clue. But sitting on a park bench in a trench coat and sunglasses in one-hundred-and-eight degree heat met me at my role-playing max.

As if stalkers didn't wear short-sleeved shirts and cargo shorts.

I'd been ready to bail on Lucas's plan completely after Ashlyn had planted one on me. She'd taken me by surprise, hugging me after I'd installed her AC unit. Then she hadn't let go. And true to form, my brain had meandered off somewhere while my body responded to her touch. To her kiss. She'd hated me for years, and suddenly she'd kissed me.

I'd thought maybe something was getting going between the two of us, but then she'd stopped kissing me and told me she'd been acting out the part of Caroline. Apparently I'd been acting the part of Andy Rich.

Damn her for not warning me first that the kiss wasn't real. It would've spared me the few minutes of guilt I'd felt over my blatant participation.

My cell phone rang. Quinn. We'd been in constant contact since Pritchard showed up. Regardless of his heroic scene with saving the mayor's son, in my opinion, the bastard reeked.

"What do you have for me, Q?"

Quinn got right down to business. "Equipment was sent and received. My contacts are already there and on target to finish installation later today. A video feed will link to your PC with footage stored on a secure channel. You'll also be able to monitor activity from your cell phone."

I heard the clack of fingers moving over a keyboard in the background. Hopefully he wasn't hacking into the CIA while I was on the line.

"You'll receive a text from an undisclosed source with instructions how to plug in to the feeds on video and GPS activity," he added. "I'm already in Pritchard's computer. Weird shit going on in there, but nothing illegal."

"You mean nothing illegal other than you being inside his computer."

"Semantics," Quinn said.

"He's at Lost Meadows RV Park, lot one-two-eight. You told your boys, right?" After Ashlyn had kissed me, I'd taken off to find out all I could about Pritchard and where he was staying. In a small town like Phair, it doesn't take long for news to travel. I'd found out he was renting an RV slip and what lot he was in within twenty minutes.

"Right. Other than this, how are things? My sister doing okay? You keeping her away from Pritchard?"

I shifted uncomfortably, trying to stir some air within the confines of my coat. Babs had asked me the same question. And I'd given her the same answer I was about to give Quinn. "I haven't exactly told her." It never seemed the right time. She'd almost found out when the local paper had done a full page article about the "hero," but thankfully, she had been in full-on writer mode and didn't see the article. She barely stopped to eat, much less keep up on current events. Didn't take much to hide the paper from her.

"That's not a bad thing," Quinn said. "Be prepared, though. She's gonna be pissed when she finds out you withheld intel."

Rivulets of sweat ran down my spine, giving me all I could take.

This playacting was fucking ridiculous.

Just as I took off the trench coat and placed it on the bench beside me, I noticed Ashlyn was on the move.

"Gotta go." Promptly ending the call with Quinn, I left my coat and followed her.

What the hell was she up to?

She wore a full white skirt that stopped just above her knees and a fitted button-up top the same shade of blue as her eyes. And then there were the cowboy boots, giving a rustic edge to her appeal. Her sexy auburn hair hanging loose in the breeze had me wanting to sink my fingers in and hang on, all while burying myself between those milky thighs. I was getting so wrapped up in sexual fantasies that could never, ever happen that I almost missed her turn and go down Main Street.

The plan was supposed to have an element of surprise. She didn't know when I'd strike, or where. Or what I'd do when I caught up to her. Well, rather, what Andy Rich would do when he caught up to Caroline.

But by the time she reached the chiseled columns of the limestone theater, Ashlyn knew I was tailing her. But rather than going into the safety of the theater's front door, she slowed her pace, headed to the rear entrance. By the time I reached the back of the building, she was nowhere in sight.

I walked up to the back door, put my hand on the doorknob, and looked around. Had she scrambled inside and up the stairs? Or had she skirted around the opposite end of the building? Before I could make a decision on which path to pursue, the knob jerked from my grasp. The stairwell door opened from the inside, and I found myself facing Ashlyn, who wore an odd expression on her face.

Before I could say something, she grabbed my shoulders and hauled me in. Her chest heaved from the effort. I waited for her to speak, tried to read thoughts that buzzed around her frenzied behavior.

Ashlyn wasn't acting afraid of me, like she should had she been playing the part of Caroline.

Was the game over?

Or was this just the beginning?

"You've been tailing me since the post office," she said, her voice different. Odd. Caroline's voice, I assumed.

"Longer than that."

Her hands slid from my shoulders, down to my chest. "Okay, so that's creepy," she said in her regular voice.

I whipped my sunglasses off and hung them by one arm from the neck of my tee. Was I supposed to be me, or Andy Rich? I threw out a line either of us would ask. "Why didn't you run?"

"I watch Animal Planet," she said. "Running is a fatal mistake. A wildebeest can't outrun a lion. The only chance it has is to stay calm and out-maneuver it."

"You're no wildebeest." I couldn't tell if she was playing Caroline or being herself. Taking a risk, I traced the line of her flushed cheekbone. I figured I'd play the part of Andy Rich. He got more action with Ashlyn—I mean *Caroline*—than I could. "And you can't out-maneuver me."

She shook her head and cleared her throat, then spoke again in her "Caroline" voice. "The police were closing in, weren't they? That's why you left New York. It wasn't to expand the family business. It was because of the mistake you made with your last victim, the evidence you left behind, the new victims still to claim."

Back to role-playing, right? But she wasn't an actress, caught up in a role, so why after I'd touched her cheek, did she start to tremble? If it wasn't from fear, there could only be one reason.

Arousal.

"There's only one thing I want to claim," I said. "And it's not a victim."

She stepped backward, but not far enough that her hand couldn't remain on my chest. "I'm not afraid of you."

I stepped close again. "Maybe you should be."

"If I said no, what would you do?"

What was she doing? Where was she going with this? Was I still Andy Rich? "If you said no to what?"

When her eyes dropped to my lips, I knew exactly what she wanted.

"If you said no, sweetheart, I would walk away, because that's what decent guys do."

Her gaze met mine.

And it hit me. She wasn't channeling her inner Caroline. "Are you telling me no, Ashlyn?"

"Caroline," she whispered.

"Fine. Have it your way, Caroline."

We moved at the same time. Our lips collided in a hard kiss. Surely this wasn't supposed to be part of the scene, but hell if I could stop myself. Her legs wrapped around my waist and stayed that way as I pressed her into a corner not visible from the alley door. My fingers sank into her sweat-dampened hair, fisted around those fiery tresses while our tongues melded in a way much different than the day before. And not just tasting, but feasting like this might be the last kiss we'd ever share. The very thought filled my chest with an ache that stole my wind. When I could no longer breathe, I pressed my forehead to hers.

She moaned my name. "Noah."

* * * *

Ashlyn

My signals were getting all crossed again. This was Andy, not Noah. Andy. But the way he kissed me, like he couldn't get enough, drained my will to stop this, even though I knew I should. I needed to re-summon my inner Caroline.

Because Caroline's struggle was to overcome her sheltered existence, facing her fears of the outside world—the unknown—I put my heart into kissing Andy again, the way only she would. And I didn't stop Noah when his fingers moved, unfastening the buttons of my shirt, nor did I stop him when his mouth covered my nipples, sucked them, one at a time, into his mouth, giving me pleasure so intense it danced on the threshold of pain. I wanted his hands on me. All of me, everywhere. I wanted him to lose himself inside me, to put out that dark fire of need that had been rising in my belly since that time years-ago when we'd almost kissed.

Alarm bells went off inside my head as his hands fought against the layers of fabric of my skirt, trying to get at what lay hidden beneath. I'd done it again. Confused Andy with Noah, Caroline with me.

"Noah," I said between kisses. "Stop, please."

At that, I would've sworn his heart ceased beating. I could no longer feel the pulse-point beneath my hand on his neck.

He cleared his throat and stepped back, too far away for us to touch. "I'm no theater buff, Wheels, but there has to be another way to get the material you need without acting out improvisational scenes for your play."

I finished righting my clothes. "Totally agree."

"I mean, Jesus, what the hell?"

"Look." My eyes locked on Noah's. The last of my control snapped. "You made your point, okay? I'm really sorry you find it all such a hardship." My eyes dropped to his obvious erection.

"You're quite the wordsmith aren't you, Wheels?"

"Isn't that why you had Lucas bring me to Phair?"

"You're really pissed about that, aren't you?"

Ignoring his remark, I walked past him and up the stairs. I couldn't believe I'd done it to myself again—that I'd allowed the lines between Noah and Andy to blur. That I'd actually felt happiness in the moment at finally getting to experience what Noah had backed away from all those years ago. Sure, we'd kissed yesterday, but that had been different from this. Way different.

By the time I reached the third floor landing, I heard Noah behind me, taking two steps at a time. Just as I reached for the doorknob, he grabbed my arm from behind.

"Hey," he said, angry, "don't walk away from me. We *will* talk about this."

When Noah spun me around, my shoulder glanced hard off the side of the door jamb. I let out a curse more from surprise than pain. I looked down at where he held me in a steel-knuckled grip. His gaze followed mine, and when I looked back up at him, the color had drained from his face.

Noah released my arm and turned away, fast. "That's it," he said. "We're done for today."

* * * *

Noah

Shit, shit, shit.

What was I thinking, getting rough and grabbing her like that? The look on Ashlyn's face, how she grimaced in pain when her shoulder slammed against the door facing, and the way she stared down at my hand that gripped her arm, ate at me. She seemed almost disbelieving, maybe even a little afraid. What I'd done had left me shaken and ashamed.

As I walked down the back stairs of The Marshall Theater, I realized I shouldn't have given in to her. I never should've agreed to act out that scene.

Ashlyn knew how to get under my skin, how to push every damn one of my buttons and yank all my chains. She heightened my protective instincts. My reactions, good or bad, became magnified. The way she made me laugh, or caused me to want to kill the person who made her cry. The way her touch lit up every part of my body. The way her kiss made me ache to possess.

More than that, though, it was the way she frustrated me, chipped away at my sense of control. Never had a woman made me want to punch my way through a brick wall the way Ashlyn Carter did. That's what made me put an end to the charade. That's what made me run.

I'd never hit a woman before. Had never even felt the urge.

Then again, neither had my father. Until one day he did.

CHAPTER SEVEN

Ashlyn

I hadn't seen Noah since he left me in front of my door the day before. With rehearsals about to start, concern for his emotional well-being had taken a back-seat to the importance of actually giving the actors something to rehearse. That's why I now stood in front of Lucas's office, waiting for him to get off the phone so I could meet with him and hand him the revised Act I and mostly finished Act II.

Role-playing with Noah had triggered my creative juices. I'd been upset when Lucas had ordered Noah and me to act out the scenes together, but he'd been right—demanding I spend time with Noah in order to connect to my muse had done the trick. The stalker scene now in the script was something to be proud of. By channeling Caroline, I'd been able to come up with the right actions paired with perfect dialogue. I *knew* Lucas was going to love the scene.

And I couldn't wait to show him.

However, not only had the improv left me nearly topless and completely vulnerable, but I'd also been on the verge of getting down and dirty in a stairwell with a guy I'd known forever but didn't even like. Since that first kiss in my bedroom two days ago, I hadn't been able to get Noah out of my mind. But that still didn't change things between us.

Just like my controlling father and overprotective brother, Noah thought he knew what was best for me. Having a hand in bringing me to Phair, shackling himself to me with party-favor handcuffs, and shoving an air-conditioning unit in my bedroom window were just the three most recent examples. What I couldn't explain was how abruptly he'd not only pulled away, but stayed away.

Finally, Lucas opened the door and I barged into his office. "Do you have time to look this over now?" I asked him, tossing the script on his desk.

Peering up at me above the rims of his glasses, Lucas picked up the pages while I seated myself on a red velvet settee.

Dressed in a mint green T-shirt and gray cardigan, he looked every bit the thin-skinned old man he was fast becoming. The issues with the theater, it seemed, had aged him over the last few months. I wondered if some of his old vigor would return once we won Best in Show.

Lucas took a seat behind his desk, and as he read, his gray eyes darted my way every now and again, but I couldn't decipher what he was thinking. Even his body language didn't give me a clue. By the time he finished reading the act, our eyes finally met.

That's when I saw the tears.

But what did they mean? Tension knotted my shoulders. Long seconds passed. His outright silence could mean only one thing.

I'd failed.

Again.

I stood. Before heading out of the office, I let my gaze make a circle around the room, stopping on thirty-two frames that were featured prominently on the far wall. Each of those frames held an autographed script or playbill from a now famous playwright, director, or actor who'd received his big break in Phair because of The Marshall Theater Players.

It had been my dream since I'd heard of The Wall of Fame, to become part of it. Judging from the look I'd seen on Lucas's face, my dream had just imploded.

"I'm sorry," I said, doing my best to ignore the voice inside me, the one that said I wasn't good enough. Then I heard the voices of my parents. My mother—perfect and blond—the ultimate society woman, setting me up to marry rich so I'd always be taken care of. Then there was my father, telling me theater and writing was fine as a hobby, but that it was time to grow up, take responsibility, and be an adult. Follow in his footsteps.

I'd failed to live up to either of their expectations. Worse yet, I'd failed to live up to mine.

Lucas straightened the pages in front of him and fastened them with a clip. He placed the sheets in his top drawer. Then he stood suddenly and came around the desk, stopping in front of me.

This was it.

The end of the line.

"Have you been interacting with Noah as I demanded?"

I swallowed the lump in my throat. Pride made my chin rise.

"Yes."

"I'm at a loss for words," he said.

I mentally cataloged my personal belongings—I would leave Phair with only what I brought—my laptop, a few clothes, and the contents of my cosmetics bag. Everything in my apartment, from the sheets on my bed, the curtains on my windows, down to the old lumpy sofa, had been borrowed either from Jess or from the prop room. I could leave a note at the Double Shot to tell Noah where to locate his beanbag.

"Ashlyn, did you hear me?"

The sound of Lucas's voice pulled me back to the present. I blinked, trying to focus on his kind yet weary face. "I'm sorry… what did you say?"

"It's working."

Light-headed, I swayed, then squeaked out, "It's *working*?"

"Yes. Which means you and Noah need to keep doing exactly what you're doing."

He positioned his hands in front of him, as if in a prayer. "In my twenty years of running this theater, *Midnight in Summer* is the most original, most poignant story I've read so far. I only hope I can do the justice in directing as you've done in writing."

I dropped back down to sitting and stared at my hands, lying limp in my lap. Had I heard him right?

"Are you sure?" I asked, looking up.

A rare grin spread across his deeply lined face. "I knew from the day we met you were something special, Ashlyn. I'm so thankful Noah pointed me in your direction. You've truly become our northern star."

My confidence soared like a booster rocket. But just as quickly, my mood crashed to the ground. What if my pushing Noah into the role-play and the scene that followed in the stairwell had given him second thoughts about sticking to our agreement? Regardless of how roughly he'd grabbed me, followed by his visible reaction to what he'd done, despite my suspicions about his upbringing, I knew Noah would never harm me.

But did he know that?

The way Noah had ended our research for the day told me he didn't.

As I rushed down the stairwell, a mixture of giddiness and trepidation warred inside me. While I was happy Lucas approved of my script, I didn't exactly know how to keep up the momentum and move forward after what happened with Noah yesterday. But maybe Jessica would, which was why my feet had taken me to her workroom without a conscious thought.

"Hey," Jess mumbled through a mouthful of straight pins when I walked in the room. A yellow tape measure hung from her neck like a scarf as she finished pinning the last of the fabric draped on the dress form. "What do you think?"

The dress was blue—a shade lighter than sapphire, with a wide plunging v that stopped high-abdomen and a full beaded skirt meant to come just above the knee.

"Pardon me for being blunt," I said, "but the woman who wears this is going to need a phenomenal rack and a whole lot of double-sided tape."

"It's for Caroline's last scene in Act I."

"The dress is gorgeous, Jess. And perfect for Caroline."

"Enough about fictional characters. How are things going with Noah?"

I nibbled my lower lip and thought of how to respond. "Strained at the moment, but I'm hoping we'll work around it for the sake of the play." I still had Act III to write.

Jessica un-looped the tape measure from her neck and tossed it on the table. "I guess Noah told you about Kyle Pritchard, then."

My gut bottomed out at the sound of that name. What on earth was she talking about? I waited, until finally

Jess looked up and met my gaze. I found myself able to speak again. "What about Kyle? What are you talking about?"

Her brows slammed together, and I could tell by the way she looked at me that she'd stepped in it big time. She pinched her lips together and looked down at the fabric in her lap, feigning interest in a seam.

This wasn't good. "Jess, you have to tell me. What does Noah know about Kyle Pritchard?"

"That the man is in town. He's one of the festival judges." Jess put her pin cushion on the table next to the tape measure, her silence saying everything.

My heart thumped, threatening to pound out of my chest. At the same time I got that tingly feeling in my extremities, making me feel light and unrooted, like this was some sort of out of body experience and not really happening at all.

Jessica's hand on my shoulder pulled me back, proving this was all too real. Though Kyle and I were both part of the theater world, our paths had yet to cross. It had been wishful thinking, hoping I could avoid him indefinitely.

"Are you sure Noah knows he's here?" I asked. But why wouldn't he have told me?

"The entire population of Phair knows he's here. He arrived with a bit of a bang. I'll show you." Her shoulders tensed as she dug the newspaper from two days ago from the bottom of her trash.

The headline read: *Festival judge turns hero to save mayor's son!*

I skimmed over the article that continued on the next to last page of the paper. Multiple photos were included, and I scrutinized every one. But it was the one taken by a pedestrian with a camera phone that held incriminating evidence. In the corner on the right-hand side of the picture, on the final page of the article, a man pulling a dolly with an AC strapped to it was crossing the street. And he was looking straight at Kyle Pritchard.

My emotions lurched from revulsion to panic to anger in a matter of seconds.

Noah Blake had been keeping secrets.

* * * *

Needing to clear my head after what I just learned, I headed out to the batting cages at the end of the city park. Smacking softballs with a metal bat or throwing fastball pitches usually helped ease the stress, but somehow I couldn't get out of my car. Instead, I sat there with the air on full blast, doing my best to keep my worry in check. Kyle Pritchard was a festival judge.

After what I'd inadvertently put him through, he'd probably want revenge. Which meant we were all screwed.

Only, what if Kyle didn't remember me?

No. That was a dumb thought.

The two days he spent in the hospital after Noah had beaten the hell out of him would've ensured I was a name and a face he wouldn't likely forget.

But the question niggling at the back of my mind was why Noah had kept the information on Kyle's appearance in Phair a secret. Why hadn't he told me?

Realization kicked in. Because of his savior complex, that's why. Noah felt it in his bones that it was his responsibility to look out for me—whether I wanted him to or not.

Well, no longer. It had to stop. Today. I'd deal with the issue of Kyle Pritchard later. Right now, I was pissed and ready to have it out with Noah. I was done being his rescue project. I picked up my cell phone and dialed.

"Blake," he said after the fourth ring.

"It's me."

"Hope you're not calling me for one of your improv scenes, Wheels."

"Not this time. I need to blow off some frustration and since you're the one to blame—"

"Aren't I always? But now's really not a good time."

"Doesn't matter if it's a good time for you. It's a good time for me. Meet me at the batting cages. At the far end of Live Oak Park, where Main Street dead ends into County."

Noah didn't respond. Instead, I heard clicking in the background. The jerk was typing on his computer, not listening. Not cool.

I pulled out my ace. "If you don't come, I'm going to look for Kyle Pritchard. Alone."

The clicking stopped. "I'll be there in thirty."

"I'm not kidding, Noah. My patience ends in twenty." Noah arrived in ten.

Tired of being cooped up in the car, I'd moved to sit on the ground in the shade. Learning Kyle Pritchard was in town ate at my gut. Discovering he was a festival judge had me freaked. And that Noah kept that particular tidbit from me as a way of protecting me had me seeing red.

With Kyle as a judge of the Phair Theater Festival, there was more at stake than ever. I couldn't trust he wouldn't be manipulative again and give us a bad review. Because spending time with Noah had resulted in such success with the script, it was imperative we stick to Lucas's original course. Once I convinced Noah that we weren't done pretending to be Caroline and Andy Rich, we'd deal with the issue of Kyle Pritchard.

But for now, first things first.

Noah eyed me cautiously, like he wasn't sure how to act when I didn't immediately unload on him about Kyle. But I remained calm to keep him off the defensive. That was the only way to get to the *real* reason behind why he'd kept the information from me.

He closed the door of his Porsche 911 Turbo, walked around to his popped trunk, and pulled out a bat bag that appeared to be a relic, circa *The Natural*. It even *looked* like it smelled bad.

"You still have that old thing?" I asked.

"Would you give up an original Rogers and Hammerstein playbill?"

I wrinkled my nose. "I'd burn it if it had that odor. I'm afraid to ask how many pairs of athletic socks died in there."

"If I'm lucky, I might have a spare to gag you with."

I shook my head. "Handcuffs and now gags."

"Hiding how you want to tear my head off under a veil of light-hearted banter isn't your normal MO, Wheels. I knew Pritchard was in town and didn't tell you. I don't know how you found out, but I understand why you're pissed." Noah dropped the bag by his feet, but kept his body shielded by the open trunk. "If I had it to do all over again, though, I wouldn't have done it any different. So forgive me if I don't apologize."

Even now, after everything he'd done, the heat of Noah's stare pulsed through me as desire for him made my legs feel unsteady when I stood. Deliberately, I took my time dusting off my rear end.

"And The Patron Saint of Assholes is back and in rare form. You are one arrogant jerk, aren't you?"

Seemingly unaffected, he gently closed the trunk and bent to pull a glove from his bag. He tossed it my direction. "If the only reason you called me out here was to sling insults, you can blow off steam without me. I have more important things to attend to."

Leaning over, I picked up the five-gallon bucket of softballs I'd rented. Without watching to see if he followed me, I headed for the batting cage, calling over my shoulder, "I can't exactly blow anything all by myself."

For the briefest moment he hesitated in his stride. "If I were you, I'd tread carefully, Wheels, or you might find yourself in a situation you can't handle."

Shame made my stomach queasy and brought heat to my face. "Is that what you think happened? You think I toyed with Kyle Pritchard, led him on in some way?"

Noah stopped just as we reached the outside of the cage. His face softened. "Ashlyn, no." He reached out to me. Fingers grazed my hair.

"Whatever, Noah. Let's do this." I dodged away from his touch, the shame shifting over to anger. Being mad at Noah felt awful, but was way better than that sickening, queasy feeling that had rocked my system seconds ago. I headed out to the batting cage, then trotted up to the pitcher's mound. Once we were in the cage, Noah got out a batting glove, bat, and a helmet, while I did one-armed windmills to warm up my pitching arm. While I was no Olympian like Jenny Finch, I'd been All District in fast-pitch in high school. Still, lacking a bit in self-confidence, I would never have had the nerve to unseat Britney Helmsworth as starting pitcher my tenth-grade year had it not been for Noah's encouragement.

"How long has it been since you tossed a ball?" he asked.

I pulled my hair back into a ponytail and shrugged.

That wasn't true. I knew exactly how long. To the day.

"Your grandmother's funeral," he said.

Damn him for remembering. And for reminding me there were times he wasn't a controlling jerk.

"You still miss her, don't you?"

An adult who thought you were never too old to stomp through mud puddles, gaze at clouds, or chase rainbows? What's not to miss? I threw a couple of practice balls and simply replied, "Yup."

The same day we buried her, Noah and I hit the cage, too. He'd found me huddled up in a corner of the cemetery, crying. Without saying a word, he'd grabbed me by the hand and led me to his car. Too upset, I hadn't argued—had just let him drive us to the batting cages. There, neither of us talked. Just rock, fire, and swing. Because right or wrong, this was where I worked through my issues.

I brushed the unwelcome memories aside and kicked the dirt on the pitcher's mound. "Batter up."

Noah stepped into position. The first ball crossed the plate so high and outside it wasn't worth the effort of a cut. The second was inside, missing Noah's kneecap by an inch. By the time I got halfway through my bucket, I'd found my groove. They weren't all strikes, but they were hittable. And Noah didn't hold back. The effort he put into his swing made it obvious.

"Are we going to talk about Pritchard now?" Noah asked.

"Keep your eye on the ball." Ignoring the bile now in the back of my throat, I threw another pitch. And another. But I could no longer keep Kyle's face out of my mind. I kept sending pitches over the plate.

Only now, with each pitch, I heard his whisper in my ear, "Classy girls do it on the first date." Felt his hands on my waist, moving lower, even as I protested.

Shudders rolled down my spine.

Dammit all, I'd finally gotten everything under control that night. When I'd stopped struggling, Kyle's hold on me had loosened. I'd been biding my time, waiting for the perfect opportunity to deliver the death kick right to his crotch. But it didn't work out that way.

Noah had arrived.

I hadn't been allowed to protect myself. Noah had done it all for me.

I wound up to throw another pitch, Kyle's face a target in my mind.

"What're you thinking about, Wheels?" Noah asked, then swung again as the pitch came at him. The ball ricocheted off the top of the cage five feet behind me.

I grabbed another ball and went through the motions. The ball sailed past his head. Then another, which went wide. "What makes you think I'm thinking?"

"You're losing control. Keep your eyes on the target."

"What makes you think I'm not?" I threw again. Damn. That ball would've smacked his thigh had he not jumped out of the way.

"Are you trying to hit me?" he asked.

Without answering, I sent another, which curved outside the plate. When Noah connected, I had to jump behind the screen to keep from getting my head taken off.

"Back atcha," he said. Then, bat in hand, he charged the mound.

Irritated, I took my glove off and threw it on the ground. "Why is it in the cage you treat me as an equal, but outside, you think I'm some weak little girl who can't hold her own?"

"You have it all wrong."

"No. I have it all right. Stop treating me like I'm seven-fucking-teen."

Noah ripped off his helmet, threw it against the other side of the cage. The bat quickly followed, hitting the fence with a clank and landing with a clatter. But this time, after his burst of temper, Noah turned to me instead of turning away. His fingers gripped my shoulders.

"Goddamn it, Ashlyn, I didn't tell you about Pritchard because I didn't want to see in your face what I just saw. On that mound you were reliving every moment, analyzing every detail. I never wanted you to have to go back to that place with him. Not even in your head." He pulled me hard against him. His hand wrapped around the back of my neck. "I shouldn't have left you alone that day," he said.

"It's not your fault, Noah."

Our foreheads touched. "I'm sorry, Ashlyn. I'm—"

Willing to do anything to stop his apology, my lips covered his and held. One second blended into the next, and the next, and the next, until finally his mouth softened beneath mine. And then his lips began to move, slowly coaxing mine open. Our tongues tangled sweetly. But what made this kiss different from the others was that it wasn't about desire, or sex, or even Andy and Caroline. This was about him and me. It was also about comfort.

It went on like that between us for what seemed like endless minutes. Until Noah pulled back.

"We can't keep doing this, Ash."

My arms, wrapped around his waist, weren't ready to let go.

"I know."

"You're off-limits to me."

"Because of my brother, or because of the—"

He cut me off from asking him if it was because of the past and instead kissed the sensitive spot just below my earlobe.

"Mmm-hmm."

Breathing stilted, I tilted my head to give him better access. "I don't tell Quinn what to do in his personal life. He doesn't tell me what to do in mine."

"This is different."

"How?"

"It just is." My hand moved to Noah's chest. "Help me find Kyle Pritchard."

He pulled away from me then, albeit reluctantly. "No."

"I just want to talk to him. Alone." I needed that. Needed to regain the strength I'd lost that night when Kyle had come after me and Noah had gone after him. Leaving me helpless.

"No way in hell."

"I need to do this, Noah. It's not your decision."

He gave one tight nod, but didn't meet my eyes. He wasn't listening to me. Noah would never listen.

CHAPTER EIGHT

Noah

Ashlyn's nostrils flared. Getting as far away from me as she could within the confines of the batting cage, she began gathering up softballs and dropping them in the five-gallon bucket. "If you won't help me look for Kyle, you know I'll do it on my own."

Now that, I didn't want. "You need to focus on the play, Wheels," I bent to collect the equipment. "Too much is at stake for you to get distracted."

"So what? I should just leave Kyle to you?"

"Did I say that?" I ducked when she threw a ball at my head.

"You are infuriating, Noah. I've known you since I was a kid. You didn't have to say it. I can read your mind."

I needed to find some way to appease her, to keep her from doing something rash, and to get back the peace we'd found only minutes before. But damn if she wasn't some kind of fireball. And damn if that didn't turn me on.

I tossed the last of the balls her way, including the one she'd aimed at my head. I needed to stall Ashlyn until I could find something on Pritchard to run him out of town. I'd deal with her anger later. "Listen, Wheels, let me look for Pritchard. We'll figure out where to go from there. The festival's still three weeks away. He probably came into town for a day or two to check things out, then left."

I should've felt bad about not telling her he'd already been found. And that I knew for a fact he'd spent the better part of yesterday looking at Internet porn. But I justified withholding the information by chalking it up to protecting her safety. I already knew what he was capable of. I only needed a little more time to get him out of town.

"Fine," she said in that tone women use to tell men it's anything but. "I'll give you three days. That's more than enough time for a man of your resourcefulness to track him down…even if he's not here."

Knowing Ashlyn, I'd better get him out of town quick. Because those three days she'd just agreed to? I highly doubted she'd honor the promise.

* * * *

Sitting in my office two hours later, I tried to focus on drafting an email to the city council regarding my deal with Cambridge Hotels, but hell if I could concentrate on anything but Ashlyn. It was the age-old conflict of wanting what you can't have, and it began long before Andy Rich and Caroline had taken root from the seeds of her fertile imagination. I'd wanted her since the day I'd found her on my doorstep after she'd run away from home.

I'd been best friends with her brother since our freshman year at Columbia. Quinn would bring me to Dallas on school breaks since I'd do anything to get away from my father. I'd watched as their father held the reins tightly on his only daughter. Hell, he hadn't just held the reins—he nearly had a strangle hold.

When she'd shown up in New York that day, from the outside looking in, I was only surprised she hadn't left sooner. The girl had brass balls, that was for sure—which was part of what I admired about her.

My cell phone vibrated with a call. Quinn again.

"Did she break your kneecaps?" he asked.

I'd texted him on the way out to the cage to meet Ashlyn, explaining her discovery.

"I'm still in one piece." For now.

"How'd she find out?"

I had no idea, but it didn't matter. "The point is she knows he's here, and she's given me three days to find him." I quickly concluded the email and hit send. One more step in the Double Shot's new direction.

"Let me make sure I have this straight. She knows he's there, but not that you know where he is?"

"That's right," I said. "Which means we need to move soon on phase two before she accidentally runs into him on the street."

I heard Quinn sip something, coffee maybe, and then he said, "I can always download some kiddie porn onto his hard drive—so far he's logged into four…hold on…nope, make that five barely-legal sites since two o'clock today. An anonymous tip to authorities would have him hauled away pretty quick."

As much as I despised Pritchard, causing him to potentially do hard time for a crime he didn't commit didn't appeal to my sense of right and wrong. If only Ashlyn had reported his crime to the cops back then. If she had, dealing with Pritchard today would be a simple matter of appealing to the festival committee and proving a conflict of interest—a conflict she'd have police records to back up. But like so many girls who'd been in her situation, Ashlyn hadn't wanted anyone to know.

At least Pritchard had left with more than just a slap on the wrist. In fact, he'd been carried out of my apartment semi-conscious by his limo driver. I'd later found out he'd spent a couple of days in the hospital after an "attempted mugging." Apparently that was the story he'd gone with.

I didn't have time to talk about this more with Quinn. Through the video feed on the security monitor, I saw Ashlyn enter the bar.

"Sorry, Q, we're going to have to talk later."

After a quick goodbye, I headed down to the main floor of the Double Shot. I found Ashlyn sitting on her usual stool at the mahogany bar, fourth from the end. She'd showered after the cage. I could tell by the ends of her hair, darker than the rest from still being wet. Her skin also had that fresh, clean glow.

Jesus. What the hell was wrong with me? Since when had I started noticing so much? And not just noticing, but committing the details of her to memory. The tiniest indentation in her cheek when she smiled across the bar as Babs handed her a gin and tonic. The smatter of freckles I knew patterned her nose. The way her grin lifted the corners of her eyes. She'd always turned me on, but this awareness itched at my skin.

Soon Ashlyn would be leaving Phair for Broadway. I needed to watch myself. Now that acting out the scenes for her play had somehow opened her up to not quite hating me as much, I worried she could end up with her heart involved. And that couldn't happen. She'd gotten too connected to me once before, and I had to make sure she didn't again. Which meant keeping the attraction I had for her under wraps.

As Babs stood behind the counter, smoking her e-cig and chatting Ashlyn up, I didn't go over right away. Instead, I stopped to talk to the handful of patrons who were beginning to filter in for Happy Hour. I didn't always get to do this, but I enjoyed it when I could. In another couple of weeks, when pre-festival events were in full swing, the Double Shot would be standing-room only on most nights. But these customers who were in the bar today were the people of Phair. They were my neighbors. Some had even become my friends.

After I circled around to Ashlyn, Babs excused herself to greet customers who'd just walked in.

"You literally know everyone here," Ashlyn said to me. "But none of them by their *actual* name."

"Not true," I replied, a bit surprised at how she'd been observing me. Of course Ashlyn had been listening to me. And watching. It was part of her job in writing her play. Gave her fodder to understand her character Andy Rich. Still, the knowledge did weird things to my insides. But at least she didn't seem pissed at me over how we'd ended things at the batting cage.

I ignored her look from hell when I replaced her gin and tonic with a Diet Coke. She never could hold her liquor, and until her script was written to Lucas Marshall's satisfaction, I considered her on the clock.

"Butch over there," I said pointing to the right, "is actually Dr. Herman Butterfield. His wife's name is Sally. They have two kids, one at UT, the other at Rice. Sally makes a mean apple fritter and heads up a knitting circle that makes blankets for NICU babies." I pointed to the pair in the corner booth by the far front window. One was a distinguished-looking bald man, sitting with a frizzy-haired woman with a kind smile. "To me, he's Daddy Warbucks. Real name is Stan Hughes, insurance agent and star of his church league softball team. Little Orphan Annie across from him is Sylvia, his wife. She's addicted to QVC."

"Why all the nicknames? I thought I was the only one—well, and Q. But he's obvious."

"I grew up in the bar business. Even as a kid sitting in a corner doing homework, it became a way to keep everyone straight. Remembering a person's name makes them feel important, but a nickname gives them a feeling of acceptance, like they're part of a club."

"Or maybe part of the family?"

Maybe Ashlyn understood me better than I did.

Something I couldn't yet identify passed between us. Then the door to the bar opened. Without taking my eyes from hers, I raised a hand and called, "Hey, Dusty."

Ashlyn turned her head, following him with her gaze. From my peripheral vision, I watched Butch pat Dusty on the back. A cloud of red dust rose into the air.

"Dusty, ha-ha. Okay, I get it," she said.

Just as she started to say something else, the front door opened again. Another regular arrived, this one a mail carrier. I reached for a pilsner glass and pulled the tap on his beer of choice.

"Hey Cliff," I said.

Ashlyn's head swiveled Cliff's way, then grinned. I sent her a wink, pleased she'd caught the *Cheers* reference.

He reached for the drink when I slid it across the bar, then took a swallow. The head stuck to the edges of his mustache. He nodded politely to Ashlyn when she smiled and handed him a napkin. "Hey, you're that girl from the theater, right?"

"One of many," she said.

"You're the writer. I remember seeing your picture in the paper. My wife made me take her to see one of your shows a few months ago for date night. It wasn't half bad."

Her grin broadened. "That's a glowing review."

Cliff wiped his face and smiled back. "It is, actually. I'm not much of a theater guy, but my wife grew up here in Phair. She and most of her family have seen every single production the Marshall's have put on since they were kids."

"I'll pass that along to Lucas," Ashlyn said. "He'll appreciate hearing it."

"See?" I said, leaning toward her over the bar. "The Marshall Theater isn't just about tourists and commercialism. It's about generations of people, of family coming together for a few good hours of mind-off-their-troubles entertainment."

Cliff nodded agreement. "Some of the wife's best memories stem from that place. My kids', too." He raised his beer to us both then headed toward his friends gathered at the other end of the bar.

"I understand how important the theater is," Ashlyn said. "But I'm not the one who walked away yesterday. Whether either of us like it or not, Noah, the improv is working. After the new material I gave to Lucas earlier today, he's more convinced than ever he made the right decision forcing us to work together."

The cook came out from the kitchen, carrying two heaping plates of nachos, one of which he gave to Butch, the other he set in front of Ashlyn.

Ashlyn dug into her food and reached for her Coke. "You know what I think?"

The way her lips closed around the straw, I couldn't keep my mind from going where it shouldn't, from wishing it were me she sucked deep into her mouth. And the way my cock stirred at the sight, I lacked the brain power to care much about anything she thought.

"The way you acted outside my door yesterday after our improv tells me Andy Rich is forcing you to face yourself," she said.

I doubted my issues were the same as Andy's.

A burst of rambunctious laughter sounded from the other end of the bar, saving me from acknowledging Ashlyn's remark. Babs had made her way that direction and stood, with one arm propped on the counter, the opposite hand waving that damn cigarette. I could tell she'd been the instigator of the noise.

"You've really found something special here, haven't you, Noah?" Ashlyn watched Babs, too. "No disrespect to your father's memory, but I don't remember ever seeing Babs this happy."

No disrespect taken. Ashlyn was right. These last eighteen months in Phair had brought Babs back to her old self, to those carefree days when I was ten—after she and my father had first married. Before things went bad.

"It was her idea to come to Phair," I said, watching Babs through Ashlyn's eyes. "Our Houston location has thrived for years. After my father's death, I started scouting for other Texas options. Babs heard about Phair while talking to some tourists one night at the River Walk in San Antonio."

That was also the night I got the call from my realtor. The Upper East Side penthouse where I'd grown up and where Babs had lived, too, had sold. Neither of us had any qualms about selling the apartment. The bad memories there out-shined the good.

When I was seven, my mother got fed up with my father's drinking and his temper. She left both me and my dad, causing the brunt of his anger to fall to me. Then Babs came along. Things got better for a while. But a couple of years after he married her, things went south again. It didn't take long before Babs stepped in, bearing the burden of his rage that I knew was meant for me. I'd forever feel guilty for not being stronger.

Ashlyn pushed her food away, pulling me out of my thoughts. When her blue gaze met mine she had that look, like she'd heard everything I hadn't said. "You came to Phair for Babs, didn't you?"

"No. Buying this location was a sound investment that matches the new vision I have for the Double Shot enterprise."

Ashlyn leaned forward. "Forget the business justification. You feel like you owe her."

Damn straight I owed her. But it wasn't the kind of debt I'd ever be able to repay.

The night I turned eighteen, I came home to find my dad going after Babs with his fists. When I couldn't stop him, I reached for the one thing that would—my baseball bat.

Babs had covered for me when the police and ambulance arrived, making sure my name wasn't affiliated with reports that could jeopardize my college admission. She'd claimed she'd acted out of self-defense.

Breaking eye contact with Ashlyn, I reached for a bottle of gin. Time to switch up the subject. "I've come up with a new recipe I think you'll like."

Aware of the contradiction I was making against my earlier statement about drinking, Ashlyn glanced down at her Diet Coke and said, "Okay."

Grabbing a shaker, I experimented with a few ingredients. Adding here and mixing there, I took the top off and poured the liquid into a martini glass. Then I sipped. After making a mental note to go lighter on the gin next time, I added a touch more lime, a ginger leaf, and slid the glass across the bar.

Ashlyn reached for the martini, inadvertently putting her lips the same place mine had been. Without even trying, the woman slayed me.

"Oh, my God, Noah." Her eyes widened with pleasure. Then she took a bigger sip. "This is amazing."

She had a look on her face, one that made my heart stutter-step and my breath catch in my throat. Then she moaned. I felt its vibration at the core of every single cell that made me a man. But even though I hadn't grown comfortable with my body's attraction to her, the eroticism of her enjoyment was more welcome than the way she'd picked at the scab of my old wound.

"Is this an original?" She pointed to her glass. "Did you make up this recipe just now?" I shrugged.

"What are you going to call it?"

I thought for a second. "Ash Thursday. I'm thinking it should be a weekly special. Once you become a famous Broadway playwright, you can write the story of how it originated. We'll print it on a plaque and hang it on the wall."

Surprise flickered in her eyes. Maybe I'd tell her the truth later—that this was exactly how her mouth tasted, citrusy sweet with a hint of spice, minus the alcoholic bite.

Ashlyn set her glass down on the mahogany bar top. "You know who gave me my first gin and tonic?"

I had a pretty good idea.

"Your father," she said. "When I was fifteen. It was my first time visiting Quinn when you two were at Columbia." Her eyes searched mine. "Do you miss him?"

By the time he was diagnosed, Michael was in stage four lung cancer. He'd gone fast. At least by then his final stint in rehab had stuck.

"He was a hard man to love," I finally said to Ashlyn. "But, yeah, sometimes I do miss him." I never would have reached peace with my father if it hadn't been for Babs. In light of his illness, she'd pushed me to work through my issues with him, to deal with the emotional trauma he'd caused. Because of her, he accepted accountability. And in the end, he apologized—and I'd accepted his apology.

That got me thinking about Kyle Pritchard.

Clearly what happened years before had left an emotional mark on Ashlyn. Maybe she needed to get Pritchard's apology in order to move on. Maybe her past was hanging up her future. And even though my gut told me Kyle was still slime, for Ashlyn's sake I hoped the fact he'd saved that kid was proof that I was wrong— maybe he had changed.

I placed my hand on top of hers, turning it palm up, and wrote the address where she'd find Pritchard across her skin. "If you have to do this alone, promise me you'll be careful," I said.

But she wouldn't be alone. Her brother and I would have eyes on her at all times. And she wouldn't know it, but I'd be there, too, at the ready in case things went south.

CHAPTER NINE

Ashlyn

Noah had come through for me. I had to admit, I'd liked it when he wrote the address where Kyle was staying on the palm of my hand. Kinda reminded me of high school. And the tingles that had shot up my arm reminded me of the same tingles I used to feel when I was around Noah. Before the whole Kyle Pritchard thing.

As I drove out to Lost Meadows shortly after leaving the Double Shot, I hoped to convince Kyle to recuse himself as judge. How could he claim to not be biased, given what had gone down between us? I never should have invited him to Noah's that night in the first place. Sure, I'd wanted Kyle's famous father to read my script—I'd had stars in my eyes about being a playwright. I'd also hoped if Noah saw me with another guy, he might realize what he'd tossed aside and profess his love for me. But none of that was to say it was okay Kyle had manhandled me and didn't stop when I said no.

I'd had so many hopes when I ran away to New York. I'd already fallen in love with the city on previous visits. What I hadn't planned on was falling for my brother's best friend. That week I spent in the apartment, with Noah looking after me, he'd been the perfect gentleman. Looking back, irritatingly so, just the way he'd promised my father. It was during a visit to Central Park that everything changed.

That afternoon, we'd been together on a picnic blanket, with me yammering about a book I was reading on Christopher Marlowe while Noah was on his back, tossing a football to himself, pretending to listen. Just as he threw the ball in the air and positioned his hands to catch it, I knocked the football away.

"Hey, what was that for?"

"How did Marlowe die?"

"Who?" Noah's brow momentarily knit, then he grinned. "I'm kidding, Training Wheels. He took a knife to the head."

I dove for the loose ball. Just as I reached it, Noah grabbed my ankle and pulled me toward him.

"Lucky guess, smarty pants," I said, laughing, kicking at his hand with my free foot.

His palm wrapped around my other ankle and he flipped me onto my back. "No offense, Wheels, but that book sounds boring as hell."

Indignant, I threw the ball at him, a wild toss under pressure that would've missed him by a mile. His hand shot up. Fingers grazed pigskin just enough to knock down the pass. And though he was on his knees, he lost balance and landed on top of me.

Without thinking, my legs wrapped around him. His hands came up to pin mine to the ground. The brown of his eyes deepened, and for a moment, I thought what I'd been dreaming of since arriving in New York would finally happen. Noah Blake was going to kiss me. I closed my eyes and waited for it to happen.

Only it didn't.

Noah released me, then stood. His back to me, he snapped out, "Playtime's over, Wheels. I'm out of here."

"Wait," I said, confused. "I thought you were taking me to a play tonight?"

"I have other responsibilities. Find someone else to play babysitter."

He took off, then, leaving me behind in Central Park.

Unsure of what happened and why, I hung out at the park for a few hours longer, crying and feeling miserable for myself, before hailing a taxi to take me back to the apartment. I could tell Noah had come and gone—not just from the utter disarray of the place, but from the fist-sized crack that had been punched in the crumbling plaster wall of the living room.

Over the course of the last few days, I'd fallen in love with Noah Blake, and if the way he acted today was any indication, he had feelings for me, too. He just needed space, time to get used to those new feelings. So I picked up the mess in the living room, taped a picture over the dent in the wall, and went to the theater alone.

That's where I met Kyle Pritchard. And had invited him back to the apartment, hoping Noah would see and would get jealous. But Kyle had gone straight from ignoring the script in my hand, to first base in a flash. By the time he went for third, I was freaking out.

Everything blurred after that. I remembered shrieking no. I remembered getting my knee poised between Kyle's legs. I remembered waiting for the exact right time to knock him in the nuts. And then Noah burst through the door.

By the time Noah pulled Kyle off me, there was no stopping what came next. And when it was over and Kyle was gone, a blood-covered Noah looked at me with what I figured was disgust. Without a single word to me, he called Babs, who'd come over and made sure I was okay. She even rode the train back to Dallas with me and delivered me to my parents.

After that night, the easiness between Noah and me vanished. He became cold, his distance a constant reminder of my stupidity and how I never should've invited Kyle back to Noah's to begin with.

I'd never heard from Kyle Pritchard after that night. For a while, he'd had a lackluster career as an actor, only to find a rousing success as a brutal, yet spot-on critic. He'd been a self-centered, arrogant asshole when I'd known him. I had to hope he'd changed inside. And that he'd do the decent thing and withdraw from judging the festival.

I pulled my car up to where his luxury Airstream was parked beneath the covering of live oaks and honked. Kyle came outside, dressed in tan walking shorts and a golf shirt, a fluffy golden retriever at his side. He caught sight of me as I got out of my car, and the false smile he wore faded. First recognition, and then hatred covered his face. That's when I realized just how very wrong I'd been. People don't change.

"Hello, *Ashley*," Kyle said.

My heart beat like a war drum inside my chest. He remembered me. He hadn't used the right name, but that seemed to be on purpose. Noah used nicknames to make people feel accepted, but Kyle had used the wrong name to demean me—to show just how insignificant he believed me to be.

"Hello, Kyle." We were past formalities, weren't we? Though he was a festival judge, I couldn't bring myself to call him Mr. Pritchard.

The dog barked, and Kyle turned his back to me to pick up a stick, which he threw down an embankment. Tongue lolling, the dog gave chase. I could hear the gentle rush of the Pedernales River in the distance.

"I know you're one of the playwrights I'll be judging," he said. "You shouldn't be here. You know it's against festival rules for you to seek me out." He caught my eye then. "Especially given what happened that night."

My arms crossed in front of me in response to his tone that brokered no apology. I tried to calm the trembling in my knees, to tell myself to not be afraid. I wasn't a teenager anymore. And I wasn't helpless.

He pushed designer sunglasses to the top of his head, making prominent a disjointed nose that dirtied up his

Waspish good looks. He didn't appear to be the kind of guy who needed to take a woman by force.

"I came here to say I'm sorry for what happened." I figured I would accept my end of the responsibility if he accepted his. "I never should have invited you in that night. I didn't know—"

His flash of too-white teeth was more a baring of fangs than a smile. "I think you knew *exactly* what you were doing. The way you came on to me proved it."

But I hadn't come on to him. And I'd tried to stop him. I really had.

Kyle had taught me something that night. From then on, I kept most men at a distance. I could count on three fingers how many men I'd allowed myself to get close enough to where sex became part of the relationship— men I'd invited into my home.

He went on. "I can't believe what you did, after all the things you promised."

My knees stopped trembling as fear got doused by a good helping of mad. "I didn't *do* anything. And I didn't promise anything, either. *You* started it. And you didn't stop, even after I said no." Pissed beyond reason, I pushed my fingers through my hair. "You wouldn't have gotten hurt if you'd done the right thing."

What had I been thinking, coming here like this? Kyle hadn't changed. He wasn't remorseful.

But that was in the past. "I'm only here to make sure our past doesn't compromise The Marshall Theater Players' chances at the festival."

At that, he glared at me, then sneered.

"It's not too late to do the decent thing. Recuse yourself as festival judge."

His lip turned up in a snarl. "The Phair Theater Festival is known for making *and* breaking up-and-coming artists. Why would I, an upstanding and well-known industry professional, bow out of anything?"

Because you tried to date rape a seventeen-year-old girl, you pompous fuck.

Those were the words I wanted to hurl at him. But I couldn't bring myself to say them out loud.

In two steps, Kyle Pritchard was in my face, only I didn't give him the satisfaction of cowering the way I might have years ago. Instead, I held my ground.

"The way I see it, *you* owe *me*, Ashlyn. You got me beat up for something I didn't deserve—something you wanted, too. I spent two days in the hospital." Kyle pointed to his nose. "Because my face is no longer leading man material, you ruined my career as an actor."

Did he really believe the things he said, or was this part of his intimidation? Kyle never made leading man because he wasn't that good of an actor, not because Noah had rearranged his face. But whatever Kyle's thought process, the conversation was getting us nowhere. I started to turn, but not before he reached out and grabbed my elbow.

"Not so fast." Kyle ran his fingers along the hemline of my short sleeve and smiled. "You're even more beautiful than I remember," he said.

My stomach soured. "Go to hell."

His eyes shot to mine as his fingers stilled. "Perhaps if you come crawling to me on hands and knees and give me what you should have given me before your boyfriend busted in, I might find it in my heart to play fair with you. I might even be compelled to use my considerable influence to see that other judges look favorably on you, too. But only if you could convince me your apology was sincere."

My head tilted, but my eyes remained on his. Was he serious? Did he *really* think…? Bile from my sour stomach rose to my throat. "So basically what you're saying is that if I sleep with you, you'll help me win?"

"As I said, I have the power to sway the other judges."

"And if I don't?"

He smirked. "I hope you like community theater, because you'll never get out of it."

I narrowed my eyes. "So, if I *don't* sleep with you, you'll ruin my career, like how you think I ruined yours?" I fake-smiled right back at him. "I'm amazed at the power you think you wield in such a vast industry."

"Ever ask yourself why *Little Lamb* never got published?"

My hand jerked, palm itching with the need to strike him. I didn't. Some people deserved an ass-kicking, and Kyle Pritchard was one of them. But I took the high road.

Kyle's smile turned vicious. "You liked it rough. I enjoy girls who like it rough."

"You like *girls*."

His smile faltered, but only slightly.

"You won't get away with this," I said.

"Because you didn't go to the police that night means I already did."

Walking to my car, I chastised myself the whole way. How could I have ever been so foolish as to blame myself for his behavior? Maybe I shouldn't have invited a stranger into the apartment, but Noah was right. Decent guys stop at the word no. Always.

"Oh," Kyle said, just before I slammed my car door. "Before you go trying to make trouble for me, you should know a very good friend of mine is a back-up judge."

Intuition crept up my spine. I knew the name he was going to say—the one I'd kept myself busy enough not to think about all week.

His tone brimmed with sarcasm. "I hear Anderson Jones has become quite a *fan* of your work. You be extra nice to me, I'll be nice to you. The offer's open, Ashley. Until curtains up, of course." He put fingers in his mouth, turned, and whistled for his dog.

Kyle may have saved the mayor's kid, but he was made of pure evil. There had to be a way to stop him from ruining it for all of us. I just didn't yet know how. What I did know was that with so much on the line—for me, for the theater, for Phair, and for *Noah*—timing was crucial.

* * * *

Upon arriving back at my apartment, still shaky from my confrontation with Kyle, I sank down into Noah's beanbag. It felt like him, the way he'd wrapped his arms around me in the batting cage. It smelled like him, too, clean and manly with just a hint of outdoors. Breathing his scent in, slow and steady, my adrenaline levels evened out to the point I finally felt safe. Ready to face what had happened, I allowed my thoughts to drift back to Kyle.

God. How dumb could I be?

Had I really believed he was capable of doing the right thing? Instead, he'd threatened me. Now what was I supposed to do? How was I supposed to escape my past?

My mind whirled with thoughts and memories. Noah, and the crush I'd had on him when I was young. Kyle, and how he ruined everything. Noah's constant interference after that night. Anger churned around inside me. I knew logically I was angry at Kyle, but instead I wanted to lash out at Noah, whose constant protective actions kept messing everything up. If it hadn't been for Noah, I wouldn't be here in Phair, facing a past I'd wanted to forget and dealing with the fact that so many people's futures were riding on my already burdened shoulders.

Stupid Quinn for telling Noah about the contract between me and my father.

Yeah, I had a bone to pick with my brother. But maybe he could help me figure out what to do with Kyle. I reached for my laptop and queued up my video chat.

Quinn answered, almost like he'd been expecting me. I chalked it up to sibling telepathy.

"What's up?" he asked, his forehead creased in concern.

I forced a smile and tried to sound breezy. "Haven't heard from you in a while. Thought I'd check in."

"Started a new project this week."

Quinn and I never discussed the particulars of his work. He was the Golden Boy—brilliant and good looking, if you liked cheeky redheads who looked like a certain British prince. He followed his dreams and our whole family cheered him on.

I followed mine and they braced themselves for failure.

The way it was looking, they wouldn't be waiting long. If I couldn't come up with a solution to keep Kyle from sabotaging me and the Marshall Theater Players, my rock bottom was right around the corner.

"Ashlyn," Quinn said, leaning forward toward the camera. "Is everything okay?"

I thought I could talk to my brother about this. Ask for his help in finding a way to keep Kyle from fulfilling his vendetta. Then I remembered how he'd betrayed me to Noah. So instead, I unleashed my gripe on my brother. "Why would you tell Noah about my contract with Dad?"

Quinn paused. "Noah's a smart guy, and he knows a helluva lot about contracts. Plus, he has a team of lawyers—some of which are licensed to practice law in Texas."

"So you showed him the contract?" My voice rose with every word. Though I knew it was irrational to blame Noah for any of this, my emotions were in free-fall.

"It was a long time ago, Ashlyn."

"It doesn't matter how long ago it was." I jabbed my finger toward Quinn's chest, visible through the screen. "You know it was Noah who convinced Lucas Marshall to bring me on at The Marshall Theater. It's because of him I'm a part of this year's festival."

"So?"

"So...if I'm that damn talented, why hadn't Lucas Marshall heard of me already? We live in the same state."

"You're looking at this all wrong, Ash. Who cares how you got in? What matters is what you do with the opportunity. I believe in you, sis. So does Noah, and so does Lucas Marshall. If he didn't, he wouldn't have brought you to Phair."

Of course Quinn didn't get it. Everything he touched turned to cash. "I have been set up to fail... To lose Broadway and my inheritance, not to mention bringing an entire town down with me."

But it was more than that. Way more. My career wasn't the only thing on the line. So was my self-respect. This had been my chance to prove to everyone—my father and myself especially— that I could succeed on my own merit.

As it stood, even if Kyle Pritchard were out of the way, Anderson Jones remained in my path. The obstacles were piling up at an insurmountable rate.

Damn, but did I ever have to write a killer script.

CHAPTER TEN

Noah

After tailing Ashlyn to Lost Meadows and back, it was nearly dark by the time I arrived at my office. Thanks to the fiber-optic noise filtering and cameras I'd gotten from Quinn and had installed around the Airstream, I was able to hear and see every detail of her conversation with Pritchard. All on my phone, while I sat in my car, fifty yards away. This allowed me to be close enough to Ashlyn to keep her safe without her knowing I was even around.

It had taken a fierce act of control not to go after Pritchard. Especially when he'd threatened to ruin her career if she didn't sleep with him. My need to wrap my hands around his neck and crush his windpipe had me shaking with unleashed rage. But I couldn't go after him. At least not yet. Once Quinn worked his magic from the surveillance end by capturing the data and putting it on disc, Pritchard would be mine. The American Theater Critics Association or other unions Pritchard belonged to wouldn't look favorably on an abuse of power by way of extortion.

Needing to calm my anger and get my mind off wanting to hit something, I poured two fingers of scotch, took a seat behind my desk, and pulled up my email. Things were looking exceptionally well with Cambridge Hotels, especially after the Phair City Council had come through and sweetened the deal with a couple more incentives. But before I could throw myself into work, an email from Quinn popped up, informing me Ashlyn had called him and was going off the rails.

I leaned back in my chair, trying to get a better angle to see from my window to hers. Besides the fact her light was on there was no movement.

A half-minute later, I stood in her hallway, knocking on Ashlyn's door.

No answer.

I heard the rattle of pipes and realized she was in the shower—her second for the day and in less than three hours—which told me exactly what I needed to know about her state of mind. Pritchard's indecent proposal made her feel dirty, and not in a good way.

I tested the doorknob and had to bite back my irritation when it turned. Damn her, she needed to be more careful. I let myself in. Unsure how long Ashlyn had been or would be in the shower, I sat on the loveseat and kicked my feet up onto the coffee table, where her laptop sat. The file for *Midnight in Summer* was open. Curious, I scrolled up to the Act 1, Scene 2 header and read. Because I knew to look, I found instant similarities between Andy Rich and me. There were also a lot of differences. We'd both been raised in well-to-do households and were the owners of lucrative family businesses, but Andy had a short fuse and an arrogant disposition that was mostly unkind.

Was that how Ashlyn saw me?

I continued reading. Andy had been the legal guardian of a younger sister since he'd been eighteen. According to the script, he still saw her as a kid, even though she was grown. One night they'd fought over his dictatorial ways. She stormed out, dying in a car accident minutes later. Andy blamed himself. But then he met Caroline at the bus stop at midnight on the anniversary of his sister's death. Andy took it as a sign—he needed to save Caroline, a perfect stranger, in the way he couldn't save his sister. Only Caroline had other plans for Andy.

The water shut off, jolting me back to reality before I finished the first act.

I closed the screen and looked up.

Steam spilled from the bathroom when Ashlyn opened the door and stepped out. Naked.

Her sharp inhale sucked the breath right out of me as the towel she'd had in her hand fell to the floor. She started to bend to pick it up, but our eyes locked. She froze.

Something in her expression changed. Seconds later and before my eyes, she became Caroline.

Slowly, Ashlyn reached up and pulled the tie from her hair. It fell in waves over her shoulders. And there wasn't a thing about her that appeared vulnerable.

She had me wound so tight it took focused effort to move. But if she wanted to play Caroline, I'd do my share and counter with Andy.

"Look at you," I said, walking toward her. Blood roared through my veins. "Backlit with steam billowing around you, you look like an angel who's lost her wings."

"Wings just get in the way."

Using my body, I pressed her back against the doorjamb. One hand curved around her breast while the other cupped her cheek. "What do they get in the way of?"

Her face turned. The tip of her tongue darted out to lick at the palm of my hand. A zap of current shot directly to my cock. Blue eyes that showed no fear bore into mine as she said, "Wings get in the way of being on my back…under you."

Jesus Christ, whether she was playing a part or not, this woman did to me what no woman ever had. My cock throbbed with the need to take her. Now. But this wasn't going to happen hard and fast like it would've in the stairwell. Being with Ashlyn was more than sex. She was more than just a body a guy could use to fulfill some elemental need. She made me want to give her everything I had. And I wouldn't stop until she was mindless.

The pad of my thumb swiped over her peaked nipple. Her breath came slow, uneven. Even though I knew I should stop because she was playing at something and I discovered I wasn't, the needs of my body usurped all logic and reason.

"I'm going to count to ten," I said, searching Ashlyn's face for a hint of someone not Caroline. I found it in the depths of her eyes.

"What happens on ten?"

"I'm going to kiss you," I said. "I'm going to kiss you until your bones melt. And that's just starting with your lips. You have until ten to stop me. Otherwise, I'm not leaving until we both come so hard it measures colossal on a Richter scale."

Keeping her eyes trained on mine, she bit her lower lip.

"One…two…three…"

Ashlyn raised the bottom of my shirt, helped to pull it over my head. Her lips touched the bare skin of my chest, sending tremors of pleasure straight through me.

"…four…five…six…"

Her fingers went to the button of my jeans. I pushed her hands out of the way and unfastened them myself.

"You're counting too slow," she said, sliding her hands down the back of my pants, inside my boxers. Ashlyn palmed my ass, pulling me tight against her. "Stop stalling. Just say ten."

"…seven…" I licked at her lips, turned with her, marching her backward to the bed. "…eight…" I kicked off my shoes. "… nine…" My cock throbbed. God I wanted to be inside her, to feel her tightness surrounding me, milking me mindless.

Her hands inched up my back. "Say it." Her lips brushed over mine. "Please say it."

I fisted her hair, but my mouth drew back, away from hers.

No. I refused to take her like this. Somehow it felt like cheating, like I'd be betraying her trust in some way. My need for Ashlyn went beyond Caroline and Andy. I didn't know what it meant. And I wasn't about to try to decipher it now. Before I went any further, I had to know if she felt it, too.

"Do you want me, Ashlyn?"

"Yes," she gasped. Her cheeks flushed, lips so red I knew they'd burn. "My God, yes."

"Say my name."

Confusion flickered in her eyes.

"Say my name, Ashlyn, or I'm out that door."

"I want *you*, Noah."

"Ten."

CHAPTER ELEVEN

Ashlyn

He wasn't bluffing. The second Noah got to ten, he kissed me so hard and so deep I lost my place in the space-time continuum. Nothing existed outside the two of us. And as his mouth plundered, his hands moved, doing the most delicious things to my body, touching me in ways no one ever had.

"My God, you're beautiful," he said, lowering me to my bed, his voice thickened by desire.

Only I wasn't beautiful. My lips were a little too big, my nose a bit too small. One breast was slightly different than the other, and no matter how many times I wore sunscreen, my freckles always seemed to multiply. But Noah looked at me like he didn't notice any of that. Seeing myself through his eyes made me feel beautiful, too.

He kissed me again, not letting up until I melted, pliant in his arms. His thumbs played at my nipples. I sighed against his lips. Then his hands moved down farther, past my rib cage, until he caressed the smooth flesh of my inner thighs. It maddeningly went on. My back bowed as his tongue traced over my breasts, sucked the sensitive peaks into his mouth, one at a time. All the while my inner voice nagged, warning me to be careful. I could let Noah inside my head, inside my body. But I needed to protect myself— keep him from getting inside my heart.

All that was easier said than done. Especially when he made me feel the things I felt now. Worshipped. Understood. Loved.

Something was happening between us. Something bigger than the physical attraction we'd been fighting recently—bigger than our shared past, Andy, Caroline, The Marshall Theater and even Broadway.

I realized I still cared for Noah Blake.

And I cared a lot.

His lips traveled lower. Fingers slid inside me as his thumb circled my sweet spot. "That's it, Ashlyn. Open up for me. Just like that."

Dear God, everything about this—about him—felt good, making me wonder why I'd ever fought against my desire. It made me wonder why I fought against my heart. But giving in to one made it possible to not think about the other. And right now I didn't want to think at all.

"I need you inside me, Noah."

"Soon," he said, positioning his shoulders between my thighs.

Then he licked me, feather-light strokes at first, teasing my swollen center of nerves, increasing the pressure of his tongue as I writhed beneath him. My legs shook as he drank from me. My back arched. I clawed at the sheets beneath my fingers. "More," I cried out. "Don't stop."

When the spasms wracked my body, he didn't wait a second longer. Maybe he couldn't. Without allowing me to recover, or even to finish, he rolled on a condom and plunged inside me.

I wrapped my hands around his neck, pulled his mouth to mine. He moaned, long and low in his throat. My hips rose to meet him. Sweat dampened our skin. As the tempo increased, I began to quiver all over again. Nails dug into his biceps. Our eyes locked.

"That's it, sweetheart," he said. "Take it. Take me deep."

And I did, giving him all I had in return, drowning in the paralyzing sparks of pleasure that shot through every cell of my body. Making love with Noah was more than a union of bodies. It was a melding of souls. And nothing in my life had ever felt more right.

As the room spun and color faded, Noah, still inside me, managed to reverse our positions, collapsing on the mattress, cradling me against his chest. Against the backdrop of the gentle hum of electric air and the wild race of our beating hearts, the world outside us didn't exist.

* * * *

I woke up alone in my bed. The sun, just beginning to rise, peeked through closed curtains. A dim glow of lamp light filtered in from the living room. The strangled gurgle of fresh brewing coffee sounded.

Last night had been incredible. I couldn't keep the smile from settling on my face, or the gratitude from warming my heart. After what happened yesterday, Noah had given me what I needed most—a distraction from thinking about Kyle Pritchard and his terrible threat. But I knew the reprieve wouldn't last long. Sooner or later, Noah would ask about what happened with Kyle. He'd think demanding answers to his questions would be his right.

I reached my arms above my head and indulged in a decadent stretch, wondering where Noah and I would go from here. My spirits deflated somewhat when I realized the answer. Nowhere. We'd come together for the sake of the play—for Broadway, my inheritance, the theater, the bar, the town. Just like how even the best shows come to an end, so too would Noah and I.

Because despite how fantastic my body felt, there was no way I could ever be with a man who acted like my avenging knight when all I wanted to do was forget about the one time I'd been a damsel in distress.

But that didn't mean we couldn't enjoy it while it lasted.

He entered the bedroom, wearing only his boxers. With his finely chiseled pecs and broad shoulders, he looked like a Renaissance sculptor had formed him of marble. A sexy coat of stubble dusted the lower half of his face.

"Good morning, beautiful." In one hand he carried a cup of coffee, in the other, an apple.

I sat up, covering myself by tucking the sheet beneath my arms. "Are you always such an early riser?"

He handed the coffee over. "I am when five a.m. here is eleven in London."

I took a sip then set the cup on the bedside table. "What's going on in London?"

He took a bite of the apple, then held it out for me. "The Double Shot is conquering Europe, one city at a time." His knee sank into the bed beside me. "Also, I promised myself if I got up, got some work done, and let you sleep, I could have you as a reward."

"That's mighty presumptuous of you." I took another bite of the apple and set it alongside the cup of coffee. "What if I'm not in the mood?"

He tugged the sheet down past my breasts. "I have ways to put you in the mood."

I reached for the waistband of his boxers, pulling him closer. "Is that why you woke me up three times during the night?"

His jaw clenched as the tips of my fingers brushed over his growing erection. "Actually, I only woke you twice. The third was all you."

I grinned. "That's not how I remember it."

"You crawled on top of me and rode hell for leather."

Acting the way I had last night was so out of character for me. But what could I do? No one had ever turned me on the way Noah did.

He pinned my arms above my head and peppered my breasts with light tickling kisses. "I remember you saying there's a pretty hot love scene between Caroline and Andy. Does she get as nasty with him as you did with me last night?"

"No." I wiggled beneath him, loving the way he grew harder in the struggle we played at. "It's a completely different context."

Noah's mouth covered mine, taking horseplay to the edge of foreplay. When he pulled away, I couldn't miss just how much his eyes darkened.

The mood went from light to serious as something inside me shifted. I brushed his hair that'd fallen across his forehead aside.

"Whatever's going on between us...." he said, "we know it can't last."

Even though I'd just thought the same thing, his words stung in a way I never would've guessed they could. Yes, Noah was right. A romantic relationship between us would never last. And not just because of my own reasons.

I suspected Noah was chasing some serious demons. From what I knew about his dad—a major drunk with anger problems—I suspected Noah's issues stemmed from that relationship. The way he'd backed away from me after grabbing my arm that day in the hall and the disgusted-with-himself look that came over his face when my shoulder slammed against the door frame proved it. Then there was Noah's admirable sense of loyalty to Quinn. I wasn't sure if he'd risk his strongest friendship to go after Quinn's sister.

Still, his words pierced at the place deep inside me that I'd fought to harden against him years ago.

"Maybe, then, we should stop with the sex," I said, only the way my hands moved over his shoulders and down his back said just the opposite.

Noah's lips feathered over mine. "What about the play?"

"Lucas threatened to find someone else to finish the play if we refuse to follow through with his plan, so…" The sheet still between us, I moved my legs, cradling Noah's lower half between them.

"It's the improvisation that gets us in trouble." His teeth scraped over my neck.

"There's also Quinn." I said. "He wouldn't like this."

Noah stopped the neck nibbling, rolled off of me, onto his back beside me. Then he took the mother of all deep breaths. "No, he wouldn't."

I covered myself with the sheet. "Then it sounds pretty simple. We have to keep spending time together until the play is finished, but not like this."

From the corner of my eye, I watched as a scowl spread over his face. "Then I guess we've reached a consensus."

We had.

No more improv, no more sex.

Last night had been all about Caroline and Andy—or at least that's how it started. But I didn't like the empty feeling I got in knowing Noah and I would never be together like this again. Seeing him every day and knowing exactly what I was missing seemed the most excruciating form of torture. Judging from the look on his face and the way he quietly gathered his clothes and dressed, I took no comfort from seeing he felt the same way.

I just couldn't see any other option.

CHAPTER TWELVE

Noah

It had been twenty-nine hours and thirty-seven minutes since I'd told Ashlyn a relationship between us couldn't last. So why was I still so eaten up that she'd agreed? Sure, agreement between us was a rarity, but that didn't change facts. The two of us becoming lovers was a bad idea—one worse than Lucas Marshall forcing us together for the sake of her writing and the play meant to save us all. The other night had been off the charts, yes, and it was an experience I'd never regret, but sometimes even the greatest experiences shouldn't be repeated.

What it boiled down to though, and what pained me the most, was that she hadn't put up a fight. In fact, *she'd* been the one who said maybe we should stop sleeping together. And when I'd gone back to her apartment after finishing the pressing matters I needed to attend to in my office, she'd greeted me by saying she was on a roll and had asked for the night off from obeying Lucas's directive. That's why I sat in my office Saturday morning, staring at an email from Cambridge Hotels like it'd been written in Sanskrit, video surveillance of Kyle Pritchard's trailer loaded on the side-bar. Within five days of Lucas's ultimatum, Ashlyn Carter already had me completely unraveled.

Without knocking, Babs barged through my office door, her forehead creased in a deep frown. "You're sleeping with her, aren't you?"

I looked up from my computer. Where the hell had that come from? "Who is *her*?"

"Don't play dumb."

"No. For the record, I'm not sleeping with Ashlyn." Which technically was true, since I was sitting in my office chair, working, and Ashlyn was across the street in her apartment, supposedly writing the script of her life. Plus Babs had used the present tense. Whatever Ashlyn and I had going, at least in the sleeping together sense, was now in the past. We'd reached a consensus. Made an agreement.

Movement on the monitor pulled my focus back to the screen. Pritchard was leaving the RV, walking to his car. I flipped to the GPS monitor, waiting to see where he was headed.

"I don't believe you. But I won't argue," she said. "Lucas wants to see you. He's downstairs. That's partly how I knew about you and Ashlyn."

I frowned. "What about Lucas being downstairs makes you think Ashlyn and I are sleeping together?"

"Woman's intuition." She inhaled slowly, letting out an equally long exhale. "That, and logic. He said it's been a day and a half since he's gotten anything new out of her. Time stamps on your emails prove you've been working…which means you haven't been with her."

I continued staring at the computer screen, engrossed with protecting Ashlyn. Then, when Babs didn't leave, I looked back up at her.

Babs cocked her head, a dorky smile on her face. "You're in love with her, aren't you?"

"That's quite a leap."

"I see the way you've been with her—the way you've always been."

I rubbed my forehead with the tips of my fingers. Babs wasn't going to let this go. "Even if I was—and no way am I saying I am—after the festival, Ashlyn will be leaving for New York."

"It's a stupid man who lets a little thing like geography get in his way."

I shook my head. "I can't go back. I run my business out of Phair now."

"No such thing as *can't*. And you can run the Double Shot expansion and the deal with Cambridge just as easily in New York. Maybe Ashlyn's the reason you *should* go back. Make new memories." Babs turned off her cigarette. "I know you came to Phair for me, son. That doesn't mean you have to stay."

I hadn't come entirely for Babs. Years ago, with the advent of new technology, I realized I could run the Double Shot business from a remote location, which meant I could build the business anywhere. Phair was as good a place for that as any. Besides, I hated New York. Hated what it reminded me of.

Her dark eyes turned contemplative. "You always get that look on your face when you're thinking about your father. That sad, unsure look. You're nothing like him, you know."

If only that were true.

"You have his business savvy, and his big brown eyes. Other than that..."

"Sometimes I snap."

"You mean like you did when you put Michael in the hospital that time? Or when you did the same to Kyle Pritchard?" Her hands flew to her hips. "Ask yourself this, Noah. What kind of man would you be if you hadn't?"

"It's more than that, Babs, and you know it."

"Michael had a disease."

She meant the alcoholism, not the cancer he later died from. "Is that why you stayed with him?"

Babs' eyes bore into mine. "I stayed because even though you weren't born from me, you're still my son." Softer, she repeated, "He had a disease."

"If that's true, who's to say I won't catch it?"

"So that's what this is about?"

I stood. "I shouldn't keep Lucas waiting."

A few minutes later, I walked into an empty bar that would be packed this time next week. I nodded to the bartender as he excused himself to the kitchen.

"How's it going, Lucas?" I leaned on the bar countertop to face the older man.

He set his glass of lemonade on the napkin in front of him. "It was going well until I stopped getting material from Ashlyn. Can you give me an update?"

I raised my brows. "No offense, but shouldn't you be asking her for this?"

"The creative process is a delicate one that I'd hate to interfere with. Per our agreement, I assume you've seen her recently?"

I hadn't, but maybe it was time I did.

CHAPTER THIRTEEN

Ashlyn

Wow. I'd stumbled on the magic formula for productive creative writing.

Sex.

More specifically, sex with Noah. Except it had been more than twenty-four hours since I'd seen him and my Noah reserves were low, causing me to fall short during the second scene of the third act.

How had we gone from me hating him to me craving his body?

I looked down at the calendar in the bottom corner of my computer. Rehearsals were starting today. With *Midnight in Summer* still incomplete, Lucas was probably stressed to the max. I had to figure a way past this that didn't involve sex or opening myself up to greater vulnerability.

Before I could dive back into my script, a message popped up on my computer screen. It was Quinn. I opened the video chat to see my older brother, grinning at me.

"You look rough," he said by way of greeting.

Ugh. Should've hit "invisible" on the chat screen. "Hello to you, too."

"Still pissed at me?"

I shrugged. "Would it matter if I was?"

"Probably not. How's the new play coming along? Finished?"

"Unfortunately, no. Just when I think I've hit my stride, there's a setback."

"Are you doing anything different now than you were doing then?"

I played dumb. "I don't think so."

"Think about it. Find the ritual and recreate it. It's what I do when I'm designing something new."

Good advice, but Quinn had no idea what he was saying— essentially giving me permission to sleep with his best friend.

I remembered Noah's reaction yesterday morning when I'd mentioned Quinn. Their friendship had been the proverbial straw that had us agreeing not to sleep together anymore. And while that straw was a valid point, in the broad light of day it absolutely sucked.

Quinn leaned forward, pulling my attention back to him.

"You said you were hung up with writing…any way I can help?"

I wished there was. Quinn was incredibly creative in his own way, but that way wasn't the same as mine. Unfortunately, the only person who could help me was one I needed in a way I couldn't have.

God, why couldn't things be simple?

"Ashlyn?"

But what if I had Quinn's permission?

"Maybe you can help," I said. "I have these two, um… characters. A brother and sister. The brother is thinking about sleeping with his sister's best friend. What do you think a realistic reaction would be?"

"Hmm," Quinn said, pursing his lips. "I don't know. I've never been tempted to sleep with any of your friends."

"Gee, thanks."

"But if it were my best friend putting the moves on *my* little sister…" Quinn made a show of cracking his knuckles.

I rolled my eyes. "Can you be serious for five minutes?"

"I'm being dead serious, Ash." His blue eyes stared straight into mine. "It would be way too weird and probably more than I could get past."

The brother giveth, and he taketh away.

* * * *

I found Jessica in the costume workroom a few minutes later. The way she frantically sliced thread and sewed on her commercial grade machine, I could tell that, like the rest of us, she was feeling the stress of the approaching show.

But that didn't stop me from unloading my burden.

In under fifteen minutes I told her about my visit with Kyle at the RV park. How he threatened to ruin my career if I didn't sleep with him, how Anderson Jones was in line to take his place if Kyle was removed as judge. How Noah had showed up later that night, probably to see how I was doing, only he never got around to asking because we ended up having the hottest sex I'd ever had—and how in doing so, I'd found my muse, blasting the hell out of the beginning of Act III and inspiring dynamic changes to the end of Act II.

I also told her how incredibly confused I was about how I felt and what it could mean to Quinn and Noah's friendship if Quinn ever found out.

"Wait, he let himself into your apartment while you were in the shower?"

I nodded. Of all the things to harp on…

"Has he not realized where he is? This is Texas. People get shot for that shit." She shook her head. "Lucky for him the only thing you're carrying is a torch."

"Ha-ha."

"Seriously, I don't get why sleeping with him is so confusing. It's just sex. Since you've been in Phair, you haven't gone on one single date."

Actually, it'd been longer than that. Almost a year, in fact. Longer still since I'd had sex.

"With that kind of record," Jess added, "it's no wonder your brain was stalled. Your system needed a reboot. Believe me, it has nothing to do with love."

I reached for her monster bag of peanut M&Ms and dumped a few in my hand. "It's confusing because I hate him…or I did hate him, and now I don't. I might truly be in…oh, I don't know!"

"You're over-thinking, Ash. To him, you're forbidden fruit. To you, he's the one who got away. It's the unknown you're infatuated with. Things will look different when the shine wears off. What you should do now is grab Mr. Sex Pistol, have some hot bump 'n grind, and finish the freaking play. After all, I can't do my job until you do yours." Jess tossed one garment aside and grabbed another. "Act now, think later. That should be the theme for the day. Not analyze the hell out of everything until you screw us all."

Jessica was stressed, like we all were. I took no offense at her down-to-the-wire testiness. With this being our third show together, by now I was used to it. "Say I follow your advice. How am I supposed to handle Quinn?"

"He said he wouldn't be able to get past you sleeping with his best friend. Handling him is easy. Don't tell him."

I put an M&M in my mouth and chewed very slowly.

"What?" Jess asked. "What are you thinking?"

No. The thought nagging at the back of my mind was stupid.

Quinn had made himself clear.

"Ash?"

"He also said something else."

Jessica finished pinning the hem on a pair of pants. "I'm afraid to ask."

"When I told him I'd hit a block, he said *find the ritual and recreate it*."

"Which means…"

"Get naked with Noah."

"Then what are you waiting for? Jump on the rich guy and pound out the rest of Act III."

Jessica ran the pants through her machine, raised the zipper foot, clipped the thread, and tossed the finished garment aside. Then she looked up. "Are we done here? Because I need to finish and you need to summon your inner Caroline."

I chucked the last three M&M's I held in my hand at her.

Laughing, she dodged the attack. "Hey, what did *I* do?"

"You're a bad influence."

"Whatever, Ash," she said, still grinning. "You came here looking for permission from someone and I just gave it to you. Now get the hell out and leave me to my work."

Just as I turned to leave, my eyes landed on a coat wrapped in cellophane, hanging from a garment rack. I recognized it by the missing bottom button.

"How'd you get Noah's trench coat?"

"It's Noah's? Lucas said he found it on a park bench—which is weird, because it's a thousand degrees outside. And also because it's Armani. Lucas thought it looked like something Andy would wear."

How right he was. I pulled the cellophane off the coat, bunched the fabric up in front of my face, and inhaled the scent of him I'd already committed to memory.

Jess shook her head. "There's no confusion, Ash. You are so gone over this guy." Then she shooed me out the door. "Take it to him. It'll give you an excuse."

CHAPTER FOURTEEN

Noah

After assuring Lucas I'd check on Ashlyn's progress, my cell rang. I looked down to see Quinn's name on the display. My mind immediately shifted to Pritchard. He'd been on the move when I'd come down to the bar. Concern over his destination had me feeling twitchy.

"I need to take this," I said, excusing myself from Lucas. By the time I reached the stairs, leading back up to my office, I answered.

"What's up, Q?"

"Are you sleeping with my sister?" he fired off.

"Whoa, whoa, whoa. What the hell would give you that impression?" Christ. Who else was going to ask that question?

"Just some hypothetical story line Ashlyn brought up when I talked to her earlier. It sounded bogus."

Ashlyn.

She'd be the death of me.

Literally.

"She's a writer," I said. "She's always working out imaginary scenarios in her mind."

"True… Besides, you're not exactly her favorite person."

"There's that." I had to get Quinn off this line of questioning before he called me out. I cleared my throat and said, "So… Pritchard has steered clear of her. He hasn't sought her out or come around the theater at all."

"That's good," he said.

Climbing the last few stairs, I came to my office door. "You and I both know that guys like him don't stay in their holes long."

"According to the GPS, he's headed in the direction of one of the local wineries."

"That should occupy him for a while at least." I opened the door to my office, feeling somewhat better.

"Look, Noah, the real reason I called is I'm coming to Phair for the festival."

I stopped short. That wasn't what I'd expected to hear. Or wanted to hear. "When was this decided?"

"I made up my mind after I talked to Ashlyn. She's my sister. If this Pritchard is threatening her career, I should be there when the play shows. I've decided to come in on Thursday."

Good. By then the play would be written and there wouldn't be any reason for him to observe Ashlyn and me together. "Can I ask you one favor?"

"Shoot."

"Don't tell Ashlyn you're coming. Not yet, anyway. It's too soon since she's found out about Pritchard. Since you weren't planning to come to the festival before, she'll make the connection I told you." A connection that would likely leave her feeling betrayed. Probably rightly so. But there had to be some way to make her understand why I *had* to tell Quinn.

Plans for his visit finalized, I hung up, then stared blankly at Ashlyn's empty window for a good five minutes. Finally, a knock sounded on my office door. When no one barged in after the warning, I knew it couldn't be Babs. I clicked the mouse over the bar's security feed.

Ashlyn, wearing a light-colored trench coat with an upturned collar and a black hat, stood outside my door.

She licked her lips.

My jeans got tighter.

I adjusted my position in my chair and watched her as she experimented with her posture while she waited.

That's when I knew that this was Caroline, not Ashlyn.

Shit.

So much for no improv.

I buzzed open the door. She entered the room, like usual. Only when she closed the door, she locked it back.

After talking to Lucas and figuring her writing had stalled, I knew why she was here. Our agreement to avoid physical intimacy was about to get blown. Time being an important factor, for the sake of the play, I became Andy, living every man's fantasy of being visited at work by a sexy woman in a trench coat... hopefully with nothing on underneath.

"I didn't order a stripper," I said, teasing Caroline in a dry tone the way I thought Andy would. "Also, I'm all out of fives."

She removed her hat and tossed it aside. Fiery red tresses tumbled down, framing a heavily made-up face that looked sexy rather than trashy.

"I like…" I cleared my throat. "I like it straight."

"Thought you liked it kinky?"

"I meant your hair, you…never mind."

Ashlyn—no, *Caroline*—walked around and took a seat, legs crossed, on top of the desk in front of me. I inched my chair back to make room. Curiosity as to what really lay hidden beneath that coat had my cock throbbing in a matter of seconds.

Running my hand up and down her calf, I said, "What happened to our agreement?"

Her hand paused over the button she'd been unfastening. "Do you want me to stop?"

Was she serious? Did she really think I'd send her away now? "Just trying to figure out what's going on in that head of yours."

"I've discovered a link between sex and writing. The more I have, the better I write." Her eyes met mine and her words came in a rush. "I know we had an agreement to not do…*this*…again because it seemed the most sane thing to do at the time, but I've spent the last God knows how many hours staring at a flashing cursor wondering where to go next, and then Quinn called. He gave us his blessing."

My hand on her calf stilled.

The color in her cheeks deepened. "Or he basically did."

I didn't believe her for a second. "How, exactly, did he give his blessing?"

"He said 'recreate the ritual.' He told me to go back to doing whatever it was that worked. That means the improvisation...and the sex."

But while her brother giving us his blessing might be a stretch—or more like a leap across the Pedernales during a flood—there was definitely logic there. And with the way her coat gaped where she'd opened the buttons, revealing the inner curve of her breast, made it feel more like a step across a babbling brook.

"When you said you found a link between writing and sex, did you mean sex in general, or sex with me?" I asked.

Her blue eyes pierced me. "I tried sex with myself. Didn't have the same effect."

Jesus H—of all the things to come out of her mouth, I hadn't expected that. Want for her sliced through me, sharp and wicked.

I pulled my shirt off as she loosened the final button, opening the coat. Inch after inch of her beautiful naked flesh greeted me. Every man's fantasy, indeed.

Stupid agreements and my phone call with her brother forgotten, I stood and pushed the coat from Ashlyn's shoulders. "Is this mine?"

"My body or the jacket?" She lowered her lashes then gazed back up at me in coquettish fashion. Then she uncrossed her legs.

"Dear God," I murmured. The woman was perfection in every way. "How do you come up with this stuff?"

She shrugged. A sly smile turned up the corners of that luscious mouth, "It's a gift. Just think of it as doing your part to further the arts and save a town."

I lowered my lips to hers.

She pulled back at the last second. "Wait, do strippers kiss on the mouth?"

"I don't know. It's your script."

"Nope," she whispered, biting at my neck. "In fact…" She made quick work of unfastening my jeans. "Drop 'em."

Once I did, she eyed me lasciviously. With clothes tossed aside, she placed her hands on my shoulders and guided me backward into my chair.

My palms covered her breasts.

She removed my hands from her body. "You can look, but not touch."

"No way. I don't like this."

She pulled out the handcuffs I'd hidden in the pocket of my coat last week. "I'm not afraid to use these if I have to." With a little smile, I leaned back in my chair.

Ashlyn dropped to her knees between mine, wrapping her hand as much as she could around my cock. She licked red lips.

Gazes locked, my fingers threaded the back of her hair and I guided her head down.

"Sweet Jesus," I hissed. From tip to stem, she slowly sucked me into the hot cavern of her mouth. Combining that with her silken tongue and her firm pumping fist, I reached the precipice of unraveling in record time.

"Come here, sweetheart," I said, trying to pull her away.

She looked up at me with those big blue eyes. "No. I want to taste you."

I couldn't say no to her. Not when the mere sight of her tongue flicking over the tip of my shaft made me want to come.

"Fuck," I growled, hips rising to meet her mouth. Moments later, unable to take any more, every muscle in my body stiffened. She moaned her pleasure at my release as she swallowed every drop.

"You're so amazing," I said, pulling Ashlyn onto me so that she straddled my lap. Her legs dangled over the arms of my chair.

"I missed you," she said.

My heart skipped a beat. That's when I realized I was in too deep.

Way too deep. As in, Crater Lake deep. The Marianas Trench deep.

I loved this woman.

I loved her guts, and her brains, and her vivid imagination. I loved her smart mouth, her passion, and yes, the fact that she was the most beautiful woman I'd ever seen. And the way she looked at me now, like the mystery of the Universe had revealed itself and she liked what she saw, told me she loved me, too.

Things might be rosy right now, but life with my father had proven how quickly it could change. And I'd rather die before I hurt her.

But I couldn't turn her away now. Not when she'd come here not only needing *me*, but needing my help— for the play, for Broadway, and for Phair.

Looking at her, so open and vulnerable, had my cock stirring again.

I locked my arms around her and took her mouth in a kiss meant to make her mine. Ashlyn's bones seemed to liquefy as she molded herself around me. Her hips circled, bringing that scorching part of her body in direct contact with the now fully aroused part of mine.

She was wet like I hadn't felt her before. Just knowing how turned on she was whittled away at my self-control.

My lips traveled to her jaw, down her neck. Her back arched as I moved lower, kissing the tops of her breasts, between them, watching her nipples pucker and darken in anticipation.

Then I feasted on her mouth all over again.

"Show me how you touched yourself," I said against her ear, "when you imagined it was me."

Hooded eyelids raised as a little smile pulled up the corners of her mouth. Slowly, she pulled my arms away, linked her fingers over the tops of mine, and placed my hands on her breasts. Her skin heated as she guided my hands with hers. Together, we rolled her nipples between our fingers until she cried out, moaning my name.

Last night I'd fantasized about watching Ashlyn touch herself, of catching her unaware and not being able to turn away. Those fantasies left me feeling a little dirty because she didn't know I'd watched or how bad I wanted her. But that was nothing compared to this reality—to feeling what she felt because she took me there with her, and in knowing that she trusted me, because she didn't hesitate in doing what I asked.

Keeping one hand on her breast, the other hand over mine trailed down her stomach, turning so that neither of our limbs was in an awkward position. Then my finger, along with hers, slid as far inside her as we could go.

"Oh God, Noah, that feels good." Her voice was raspy, her breath ragged.

I'd never experienced anything so erotic as watching her, feeling how her insides swelled around our aligned digits. My cock throbbed with an urgency to take her slow and deep.

Sensing my need, Ashlyn pulled out. Using the arm rests, she braced herself, raising her hips as I positioned myself between her thighs. Then slowly, she lowered, fitting tight around me like her body had been tailor-made for mine.

"Noah," she moaned, working her hips exactly the way I liked. Watching her move in synch with my upward thrusts was like poetry—a perfect sonnet of unmatched beauty that let me know, with her, anything was possible. That being with her offered something better than love.

Something that felt a lot like redemption.

Ashlyn kept a firm hold on her release, waiting for me, I knew. And when the quivering started in her belly, moving through her limbs, I wasn't far behind.

"Come on, sweetheart, let go. Come for me."

Our eyes locked and my mind blanked. Spasms ripped through her seconds before the rolling wave of my own orgasm knocked me flat. I'd never experienced anything as mind-blowing, nothing as intense.

Burying my face into the curve of her neck, I pulled her hard against me. Her fingers of one hand threaded my hair. With the other, she traced along the line of my jaw.

"Kiss me, Noah," she whispered. "Kiss me like I matter." My head dipped. Her ragged breath fanned my face.

Our lips locked.

And yes, I kissed her. I took her mouth the same way I took her body—slow and sensual—like she mattered. Because whether I liked it or not, she damn well did.

CHAPTER FIFTEEN

Ashlyn

It had been a risk coming to Noah this way. One I'd been willing to take for the sake of the play, even if it was at the expense of my heart. Based on the ideas already swirling in my head, vying for a spot on a page, I knew that risk was going to pay dividends.

"You lost your shoes," Noah said, holding my stilettos by the heels. He followed that by saying, "Leave the coat. I'm thinking of having it bronzed."

"Very funny." I slipped my arms in the sleeves. "If you have it bronzed, we can never use it again."

His brows rose as he set the shoes aside and finished fastening the buttons on his jeans. "Okay, but I still want the coat back… someday."

I picked up one of the shoes, bent my leg behind me, and slipped it on my foot.

"Lucas was here," Noah said. "Right before you."

My gaze dropped to the other shoe. "Let me guess. He's concerned because I haven't given him anything in over a day and a half."

Noah nodded.

Just great. Noah had questioned my seeking him out, but he hadn't resisted in the slightest. While the part about sex between us having a positive effect on my writing had been true, he'd accepted my thin link between recreating rituals and Quinn's unspoken blessing of our relationship—a fact that sent my heart down a path of hope. But Noah having talked to Lucas prior to my arrival explained everything. He'd been acting as Andy as much as I claimed to be acting as Caroline, making that path a dead end trail. Even the way he kissed me at the end probably hadn't been real.

"Wheels, look. What if we're making this more complicated than it needs to be?"

"How do you mean?"

"If sex is what you need…"

"I know what you're getting at. Sex confuses an already weird situation, and neither one of us intended to take it there. The fact that it helps my writing is something I don't like any more than you do."

"Don't like it?" Noah snorted a laugh. "Could have fooled me."

"I don't like the *complication*. The sex is…" Unable to help myself, I let out a dreamy sigh. Then I noticed Noah looking at me, a self-satisfied smirk on his face.

What an ass. The smugness was entirely uncalled for.

I cleared my throat and started over. "After everything that happened the other night, I wrote. And not only did I write, but it's *really* good. Better than what Lucas read before."

"So what you're saying is that sex with me blew the cobwebs out."

"In a manner of speaking."

Noah rubbed his jaw. "And what you're getting at, without really saying it, is that I need to suck it up and take one for the team."

I half-smiled.

He took a step forward, crowding me with his body. "You don't know how hard this will be for me, Wheels."

"Pun intended?"

"When you hit the cover of *The New Yorker*," he said, backing me against the door, "I better get some recognition."

"I'll dedicate my two-page spread to you."

Noah's hand found the opening in my trench coat where a button should have been and slid a hand up the inside of my thigh. "You'd better."

Desire pulsed through me as his touch inched closer and closer to the hidden place that longed for only him. And then he pulled away. The tease.

"Okay, then, since you say we sort of have Quinn's blessing, we'll do this for the play."

"And when the play's written…"

"We stop."

Noah and I had finally come to a new and workable agreement, but dread lined the pit of my stomach. The more time Noah and I spent together, the more we became Caroline and Andy…or vice versa. And this was the part in the story where the very thing that brought my characters together also tore them apart.

"Before it goes any further," Noah said, "there's something we need to talk about."

My head rolled against the door. This couldn't be good. "What?"

"Pritchard. It's time you tell me exactly what happened between the two of you the other day. And I mean everything."

My body tensed. "Noah, I'd really rather not." "His being here isn't a coincidence."

It wasn't.

Kyle was out for revenge.

Noah backed off me, as if he realized I needed some space, and poured us both a drink from his personal supply. I took a seat on the leather sofa.

"I respected your privacy on this for as long as I'm going to," he said, handing me a glass of scotch. "Now it's time to talk."

Given how volatile he was where my safety was concerned, spelling out Kyle's threats seemed counter-productive. When Noah saw red, he had a tendency to lose control.

Considering Noah had told me how to find Kyle, I felt I owed him full disclosure. But as I watched his facial expressions, and his body language in reaction to what I said, something inside told me Noah already knew.

"Nothing happened," I said, standing.

Noah stood, too. "Ashlyn—"

"I handled it." My chest squeezed tight as I walked out.

Brushing past him, I added, "That's all you need to know."

* * * *

Holed up in my apartment, sitting on Noah's beanbag three hours later, I sensed something still off with the play—which was odd considering the amazing sex I'd just had. Regardless, the character of Andy had changed ever so subtly, and I couldn't put my finger on how or why.

Maybe it was Noah and the wall I sensed had gone up after we'd made love. A wall I had no idea how to tear down.

Or did I even want to? Walls might be better…for both of us.

A walk around the park might do me a world of good. I needed fresh air, anyway. Something other than Noah's last beer in my fridge wouldn't hurt, either. I made a grocery list and put on my tennis shoes.

The thick scent of rain greeted me when I stepped outside The Marshall Theater. A storm blowing in from the north brought with it cooler temperatures and a welcome cover of clouds.

Preparations had already begun for the annual festival and kick-off parade. Shopkeepers busied themselves by sprucing up window dressings, hoping to entice tourists to buy souvenirs. Lights strung through live oaks would soon be added, and the burned out M on The Marshall Theater sign had been replaced yesterday.

I spotted Lucas, sitting with Babs in the park pavilion. They looked deep in conversation. Debating whether or not to interrupt, I headed that direction.

"Ashlyn," Babs said. She darted a glance at Lucas, who looked visibly upset.

"Hi Babs," I said. "Lucas, is everything okay?"

With a shaky hand, he pulled a handkerchief from the pocket of his cardigan and wiped at watery eyes. "I should tell you now, Ashlyn. You probably need to gather your things. City inspectors came by this morning. They're concerned about liability should something catastrophic happen. They're thinking of closing the theater before the festival."

My heart dropped. "What? They can't do that. The festival is as important to the town as the theater is."

Babs reached over and placed a comforting hand on his knee.

"They're concerned about fire risks to an over-taxed electrical system. There also appears to be structural issues with one of the balconies."

Shell-shocked and numb all over, I asked, "When will we know for sure?"

"City engineers and the county fire marshal are weighing the options. It will be another week before we get an answer. If the theater is closed down, it's possible the festival could be cancelled."

I dropped to the bench beside Lucas.

"Considering the danger of fire," he said to me, "I think you should gather your things and move out."

Move out? Where would I go? I thought about the little bit of padding I still had in my bank account, and how quickly three weeks in a hotel would run it up.

"If you need a place to stay, Ashlyn," Babs said, "you can stay with me."

"No," Lucas said. "She should stay with Noah. It only makes sense, considering the play isn't finished."

Finding out I didn't have AC, Noah had ordered me to stay at his house. Now that I was essentially homeless, I didn't think he would turn me away.

Movement behind a tree caught my eye. I turned to see a golden retriever fetching a tennis ball. The dog ran and dropped the ball at his master's feet. Kyle Pritchard looked up. A grin slowly spread across his face. I quickly turned my back on him. No way would I let that jerk see me sweat.

I shoved off, leaving Lucas and Babs alone, and headed to the open-air market at the opposite end of the park. The clouds in the sky darkened just as I felt a presence behind me. The obnoxious scent of French after-shave surrounded me in a fog. I fought back a gag.

Kyle.

"Peaches are good this time of year," he said. "There's something else I imagine tastes a lot like peaches."

Refusing to acknowledge his disgusting comment and what I could only presume to be his meaning, I said, "This is against the rules, Kyle."

He stepped closer. "I overheard Lucas Marshall, crying to the barmaid. Haven't you small-town people learned how the real world works? An envelope full of cash handed under the table to the right city official will ensure the theater remains open for as long as it's needed."

"Are you saying Lucas should stoop to bribery?"

"It's just a suggestion. I'd hate to have come all this way for nothing."

"Is that how you paid for that expensive Air Stream and over-priced aftershave?" I snapped out. "Do people pay you for positive reviews?"

"Do I hear wishful thinking in your tone? You think your rich boyfriend can buy you a spot on Broadway?"

Stepping around him, I searched the market for a fruit or vegetable that couldn't be used for sexual innuendo. I found it two tables over in the asparagus. Unlike the peaches I'd loved but would never be able to look at without revulsion again, the asparagus seemed safe.

"I always play fair. And so does Lucas Marshall. If there's legitimate danger, he'd never put people's lives at risk."

"Whatever you say, Ashley," Kyle added. "Like I said, I'd hate to have come all this way for nothing. But if it's Broadway you want, perhaps we could make an arrangement with or without the festival." His dog, tied to a nearby tree, barked. Kyle stepped that direction. "My offer's still open."

I swallowed my revulsion as I watched Kyle cross the park. A gust of cool, shivery wind followed as he walked away.

* * * *

A while later I walked back into the Double Shot. At the bar, Dusty and Butch turned and caught sight of me. "Hey-hey, Training Wheels," one said, while the other let out a whistle.

I self-consciously waved. My gaze darted between them then narrowed when Noah stepped out from his hiding place behind the two.

Should've known he'd put them up to it. I went to my usual stool and took a seat. Noah handed me a drink.

"I need a favor." I pushed my drink aside, leaned across the bar, and cleared my throat. "I'm getting kicked out of my apartment."

His eyes narrowed, trying to figure out how that could be. "Did you not pay your rent?"

I explained how I'd run into Lucas and Babs at the park and the city inspectors' findings. "I can probably stay with Jessica. Babs even offered. Of course Lucas thinks you are the best alternative. He's so freaked out right now I didn't want to cross him."

Noah scratched his chin. "If memory serves, I recall a similar offer made recently that was thrown back in my face."

"Once again, your memory is skewed. It wasn't so much an offer as an order."

He leaned in. His finger traced along the pulse point on the inside of my wrist. "What do I get in return?"

I tilted my head, offering my best smile. "Besides a chance to keep your bar and your town and your big expansion deal with Cambridge Hotels?"

"Looks like we have ourselves quite a conundrum."

"Why is that?"

"Quinn wouldn't want you sleeping in my bed any more than he would want you sleeping in your car. If you stay with me, Ashlyn, you will be sleeping in my bed. At least, until you finish the play."

I reached for my drink. "Thing about that is, writers aren't done until the show's had its run."

Noah trying to hide his smile only made his mouth irresistibly sexy. "Guess that's lucky for me."

Butterfly wings fluttered against my stomach as that old familiar tug pulled on my heart. Unlike him, I couldn't hold back my grin any more than the wistful little sigh that escaped.

He tossed me a set of keys. I caught them mid-air.

Game on.

After packing up my car and following Noah's directions to the letter, I drove down an oak-lined lane, six miles outside of Phair, until I reached Noah's house. Set in a valley between rolling hills, the rounded edges of the landscape softened the sharp corners of the house's stone pillars. I parked my car in the garage, punched the code to deactivate the alarm, and traveled through the wide archway to a side door.

The hairs on my arms rose as I went from room to room. Inspiration in the form of sex wasn't what I needed from Noah, at least not today. It was this—seeing who he was when no one was watching.

Though small colorful rugs graced them, hardwood floors were otherwise bare. Walls not made of glass were spartan. Architecturally, the house was stunning, but it was an empty shell. It had no soul.

I continued to wander through the rooms then let myself out to the hidden sanctity of the enclosed sun porch. The second I stepped through the door I felt the essence of Noah surround me. The house might be empty, as if waiting for someone to live in it, but not this space. Various photographs of Noah with his friends from Phair lined a low table. A chenille throw lay bunched up on an antique metal bed, with a book lying face down on top of it. I ran my fingers along the book's threadbare cover first before picking it up.

Henry David Thoreau. Based on the worn, dog-eared pages and highlighted passages, he'd read Walden a lot.

A smile tugged at the corners of my lips. Just when I thought I had him mostly figured out, he threw me a curve ball.

He loved Phair. That much was true. And because of his turbulent family life, part of him probably even needed the calm pace, the loving support of a tight-knit community. Even though he was a businessman who wouldn't hesitate to cut his losses and move on if it came to it, I had a strong sense he didn't want to. Phair was his family now.

Kyle Pritchard wasn't just putting my career and The Marshall Theater at risk. This wasn't just about saving the town of Phair or Noah's big expansion plans with the Cambridge Hotels. Kyle's threat would destroy what was now Noah's family. And there was nothing I could do to help.

CHAPTER SIXTEEN

Noah

It had been difficult not to let on to Ashlyn that I knew about her run-in with Pritchard. While I knew because of the GPS tag I'd affixed to his dog's collar that he was at the park, if it hadn't been for Babs, I wouldn't have known Ashlyn had been there, too, or that he'd followed her. Unfortunately, the view out my office window didn't extend that far.

Somehow I had to find out what he said without raising Ashlyn's suspicions. Quinn was right. She'd be pissed as hell if she found out about the surveillance.

But all that had to wait in line behind a more pressing emergency. City inspectors couldn't be serious about closing down the theater before the festival. The very idea was asinine. It prompted me to reach out to Haywire. As soon as he emailed me a copy of the inspection report, I looked it over.

"We can slap a bandage on every issue except electrical," Haywire said over the phone. "With these old buildings and all their sub-panels, there's no way to isolate the problem without tearing through walls. Best I can tell you is we'll know more once the fire marshal comes back with his ruling."

The fire marshal's ruling was what worried me. Still, after seeing Haywire's preliminary report, I had faith I could convince the fire marshal to agree to terms that benefitted the town, without putting anyone in jeopardy. On Monday morning, I'd make an appointment and present this plan.

But right now all I wanted to do was get home to Ashlyn. Since it was long past nine on a Friday night, hours since I'd last seen her, it occurred to me her well of inspiration might need to be tapped. My pulse jumped at the thought. Fire dangers and Lucas's notion that Ashlyn and I should stay glued at the hip were proving to have advantages.

Heavy rain turned a ten minute drive into twenty, and soon I was home. I didn't like how anxious I felt. Having someone to come home to wasn't a feeling I was accustomed to. Neither was I accustomed to looking forward to it.

The minute I opened the door leading from the garage, the sound of Eddie Vedder on the sound system greeted me.

I followed the trail of Ashlyn.

Keys left on a console table. Her purse dangled from a door knob. A hair tie with a few strands of hair still stuck to it had fallen to the floor. Off to the side, in the living room, I glimpsed my beanbag. The stack of scripts she'd kept in her bedroom had toppled over beside it.

She might've left her apartment, but the chaos of it followed. Oddly, I wasn't irritated by the mess.

When I found her, she was standing at the kitchen island, hips swaying to the rhythm of the music as she sipped from a glass of white wine, adding toppings to a homemade pizza. Suddenly she stopped, reached over, and typed a few lines on her open computer. Then went right back to the pizza. I stood back and watched, thinking of all the ways I could use that island—ones that maybe included food, but had nothing to do with cooking.

Sensing my presence, Ashlyn looked up. When she saw me, she smiled. "Hey," she said. "I kinda made myself at home. Hope you don't mind."

"No," I replied, my voice sounding thick, hoarse.

"Basil, or no?"

I cleared my throat. "No."

She added some to only half the pizza. That done, Ashlyn turned to slide the pan into the oven, giving me a nice look at her ass in the tennis skirt she wore. Then she stepped over to the fridge, reached for a beer, twisted off the cap, and held it out to me.

All at once, fifty years of nights just like this flashed before my eyes—of coming home from a long day and finding her cooking, or working, or daydreaming. Of shared dinners and kids doing homework at the kitchen table.

I'd thought coming here, to Phair—having this secluded space, this peace—was all I'd ever need.

That was before Ashlyn came to town.

The one person I could never have was the only one who could set me free. But the cost of freedom was more than I could spare. I'd never jeopardize Ashlyn's safety for anything. Thanks to Michael contributing half my DNA, being emotionally involved was too risky. I'd already proven that to myself, once with my own father and once with Pritchard.

Her smile faded. "Noah? What's wrong?"

I raked fingers through my hair with one hand and set the bottle down on the counter. "Everything's a mess, Wheels."

"I know, but don't worry, I'll clean it up."

She thought I meant the kitchen. I walked around the island, then wrapped my arms around her waist as she put dishes into the sink. "That's not what I meant."

"Do you mean the festival set-back?" She turned her head to look at me over her shoulder. "I assume Babs told you."

My action, going to her the way I had, holding her in my arms, had been natural. Without thought. But it was also too intimate a gesture—what a husband would do. So I released her. "I talked to Haywire—the city's electrical engineer—he says the fire danger is the sticking point. I'll take care of it Monday."

She turned to face me. "You sound confident."

"Haven't found a problem yet, I couldn't fix."

Thunder cracked, rattling the windows. Ashlyn jumped. She'd never liked storms.

I stepped toward her again, my instinct to protect her strong, but instead of taking her in my arms like I wanted, my hand came up to caress her cheek. I couldn't *not* touch her. Not when all I wanted to do was hold her until the storm passed. But that would only send the wrong message.

"Quinn is coming for the festival," I said. Even though I'd asked him not to tell her, I'd grasped at anything that would put emotional distance between us.

Ashlyn's brow wrinkled. "Quinn? Why?"

Rather than confess to spilling her secret to her brother, or spilling mine about Pritchard's surveillance, I took another angle. Something I was sure wasn't a lie.

"He wants to see your play."

"Why didn't he tell me that when we talked?"

I shrugged. "Guess he wanted it to be a surprise. Or I don't know, maybe he decided *after* you talked."

She let out a slow breath. Our eyes met. "That means he'll be staying here."

I nodded.

"So...we pretend like nothing's happened between us?"

"Do you have a better idea?"

For a split second, her shoulders slumped. "No, I guess not." Her spine stiffened, and she turned to the dishes.

I hated that I hurt her. But what did she expect? We'd painted no illusions this would be permanent.

Ashlyn scraped leftover vegetables from the cutting board and washed them down the disposal.

"It would be stupid to ruin a decade long friendship on my account," she tossed out.

I reached for my beer and took another drink. "What do you want from me, Wheels?"

"Nothing, Noah."

She dropped a knife into the sink with a thunk, telling me *nothing* was definitely *something*.

"I knew this was a mistake," she said. "What am I even doing here?"

"The theater is a death trap. The play isn't finished, and you staying here is what Lucas wanted."

Did I need to remind her she was fighting for a spot on Broadway, not to mention a whole lot of money in the form of her grandmother's legacy? Of course I couldn't say the one thing I wanted to, the one thing that mattered most. *You're here because I want you here.*

"What if I told you the play's finished?" she said. "That I emailed the final draft to Lucas two hours ago? What would you say to that?"

I took another pull on my beer. "You said it today. Writers aren't done until the show's had its run."

CHAPTER SEVENTEEN

Ashlyn

Of all the words to come back and bite me, I never thought it'd be those.

I tossed the dish cloth in the sink, closed the screen on my computer, and without making eye contact with Noah, proceeded toward the sun porch.

"Where are you going?" he asked. "Smells like the pizza will be ready in a few minutes."

I wasn't hungry anymore. And I didn't owe him answers. Without turning back, I kept on going.

"Ashlyn," he called. His tone wasn't harsh, but it wasn't pleasant, either. When even that didn't get a reaction, Noah moved. He bolted in front of me, blocking my path. "Don't walk away from me."

That day in the stairwell flashed through my mind. Noah grabbing me from behind, my shoulder smacking against the door frame, how he'd looked, thinking he'd hurt me.

"Why, Noah? Why shouldn't I walk away? After all, you always are."

"What are you talking about?"

"You had the same reaction that day in the stairwell, after our first improvisation. I thought it was because of your father and his abusive tendencies. How you think you might turn into him."

"You don't know anything about that, Ashlyn."

"We've known each other a long time, Noah. No one had to say anything for me to know. Funny thing is, I've just realized it's not about him. It's all about control and who has it. You can walk away from me, but I can't walk away from you."

"It's about common courtesy, Wheels. Can we not simply share a meal together after you went to all the trouble?"

I stepped around him, walking out onto the porch. Catching up to me, he reached for my arm, his touch gentler than it had been that day in the stairwell. "Ash."

"You think you have to control every situation."

Noah shook his head in slow denial.

Could he not see what he was doing to me? That my heart broke a little more each time he pushed me away? I still couldn't look at him. "You use Quinn as a barrier between us. He's your excuse when you need distance."

"If that's what you think, I don't see it." His hands flew to my cheeks, forcing my gaze to meet his. "I need distance because I can't tell what's real between us anymore. Are you Ashlyn or Caroline? Am I supposed to be Andy, or Noah?"

My heart constricted like it had been crushed in a compactor. My throat closed up. I struggled to speak. "After today, in your office, you can honestly say that to me? That you don't know what's real?"

If only we would've stuck to the script during those times we acted out possible scenes—kept our time together strictly about Andy Rich and Caroline, we wouldn't be having this conversation. But no, from the first time we made love, he'd crossed the lines, insisting that it be between us, not them. And he had the nerve to say he didn't know what was real. Well, maybe it was time I told him. Put it all out there. After all, holding it in wouldn't be playing fair.

"I love you." I said. "That's what's real. And I don't know what happens next, but I don't have to. I just need to know you're willing to work it out because I know you feel something for me, too."

Jaw tense, Noah searched my eyes, and in his, I saw confirmation. He really did love me, too.

"Tell me you love me, Noah."

The tension in his jaw slowly softened. That's when he stepped forward and kissed me, languid and sweet. It was a direct contradiction to the pent-up edge I felt in his body, further proof that he wasn't his father. That he'd mastered control of his physical actions. And once again, this kiss was different than the others. It wasn't about possessing, or lust, or even comfort. It was about giving me what he thought I needed.

As much as I wanted to lose myself to him, to follow the lead of my natural instincts and his, I couldn't. Not when it would make the pain of parting that much more unbearable. And not when he was trying to say with his body what he struggled to say with words.

If only I didn't *need* the words.

I stroked his hair. Wrenched my mouth away. Then rested my forehead against his. "Tell me you love me," I breathed.

"You need this play to be a success as much as I do," he said.

"The only way that happens is if we work together."

"Tell me, Noah."

Why wouldn't he just say it?

Thunder rolled. Lightning illuminated the night sky. I swallowed the knot in my throat. Our eyes met, and for a second I saw everything he'd struggled to suppress. The expression he wore was the exact same expression he'd had that day in Central Park.

He loved me.

There, in that look, was proof of what I'd somehow always known.

Hope surged inside me. The daunting obstacles that stood between me and Broadway, my inheritance, and saving the town, suddenly felt achievable. All Noah had to do now was say those three small words and I'd be his forever.

"Say it," I said, breathless.

A flash of lightning hit its mark nearby. Noah remained silent. Thunder cracked, right along with my heart. Tears welled, but like a heavy cloud couldn't stop the fall of rain, I couldn't choke back my pain.

Noah's hand went to my chin, forcing me to meet his eyes. "Ashlyn, don't do this."

The realization he wasn't going to say it hit me like a punch in the gut, knocking out my wind, leaving me hollow and broken.

He dropped his hand, gazed at me for another long moment. His lips went tight. His face harsh. Then he turned his ramrod-straight back to me.

And walked away.

Leaving me alone, just like I knew he would but had hoped with everything inside me he wouldn't. A chill that felt a whole lot like regret settled in the air. A blast of wind from the north gusted, taking down a limb from a hundred-year oak. It snapped then tore, and when the lightning illuminated the sky again, it revealed the tree's insides as shredded as my own. But the limb continued to hang by a thread, until finally it crashed to the ground.

Was that what I'd been doing all these years? Hanging on to that shred of hope? Blaming my inability to love and to trust on Kyle Pritchard, when it really all hinged on the fact that whoever I was with wasn't Noah?

"What the hell's going on here?"

I whipped my head around to see my brother standing in the doorway.

Surprised, Noah looked up the same time as me. Then he wiped the back of his hand across his mouth. "Q, what're you doing here? I wasn't expecting you until—"

"I didn't trust the mail." Quinn tossed what looked to be a thumb drive at Noah, who caught it with one hand. "Never thought it'd be you I couldn't trust."

Thunder rattled the windows of the enclosed sun porch again. The lights flickered off, then on. Chill bumps rose on my spine. "What's that?" I asked, looking from Noah, to Quinn.

A vein in Quinn's jaw throbbed. "It's Noah's grand plan to get Kyle Pritchard out of your life for good. Didn't he tell you about it?"

I looked at Noah again. He'd had a plan about Kyle?

Quinn added, "Guess he's good at keeping secrets from both of us."

What was Quinn saying? That Noah had gone behind my back and colluded with my brother? Trying to keep myself from doubling over in pain and shock, I wrapped my arms around my waist. My eyes leaped to Quinn, who kept his gaze on Noah. Finally, I managed to get words out. "What do you know about Kyle Pritchard?"

"Ashlyn, I can explain," Noah said.

"On the subject of Pritchard, anyway," Quinn said. "He told me all I needed to know."

I'd been so sure I could trust Noah, especially with this, of all things. Hurt and betrayal washed over me at once and kept me from breaking down. I held my hand out to Noah. "Give me the thumb drive."

"Could you give us a minute, Quinn?" Noah said.

"No," I said, answering for my brother. "What's on the flash drive?"

"Surveillance." Quinn glanced at Noah. "I told you she'd be pissed."

My gaze snapped to Quinn's. "Oh, just shut up. Forgive me if I can't possibly believe you were an innocent lackey."

I walked over to Noah and snatched the device from his hand.

The fingers of his other hand moved to my waist. "We're gonna talk about this, Ash."

"Oh, *now* you want to talk," I spat out, pain fueling my anger. "I don't think so. You saw me at Kyle's that day, didn't you?"

Noah's level gaze didn't back down from mine as more tears spilled down my cheeks.

"All this time I was so worried about you being afraid you'd turn into your father. Until now, I never realized how much you'd turned into mine." I gathered all the bravado I could muster and straightened to my full height. "Your part in this play is over, Noah. On behalf of the citizens of Phair and The Marshall Theater, thanks for taking one for the team. How does it feel to be right? There really is no problem you can't fix."

CHAPTER EIGHTEEN

Noah

She didn't even wait for the storm to subside. Ashlyn left for Jessica's, and all I could do was stand back and watch her go. When I could no longer see her taillights from the wall of front windows, I joined Quinn in the kitchen.

He handed over one of two beers he'd pulled from the fridge. "Seeing you all hang-dog is going to take the fun out of kicking your ass."

"Mind if we save it for another day?"

Quinn took a long drink from his beer. "Do you love her?"

"More than you know."

He let out a solid string of expletives. "I knew this was going to happen. The second you told me she was coming to Phair, I knew it would come to this." He shook his head in disgust. "Noah, what the hell were you thinking? You know she's been hung up on you since she was a kid."

Beer raised, I stopped it four inches in front of my mouth. "Actually, I didn't." I took another drink. "And what I was thinking was she's my best friend's little sister who I promised to always look after."

"A promise once made is never broken," Quinn said, reciting our old fraternity pact. "That's quite an excuse."

"She turns twenty-five in just over a month, so I was also thinking about the contract your father coerced her to sign, and that if she came to Phair, she'd have a good shot at keeping her inheritance, have a legitimate chance at Broadway, and maybe save the theater that's been in a family for five generations." I drained the rest of my beer. "So forgive me. She's been here for seven months and I hadn't laid a hand on her. Why would I think the past five days out of two hundred and fifteen would be any different?"

"Wow, now that you spell it out in plain English, I don't know how I missed it," Quinn said, shaking his head. "You are one arrogant sonofabitch."

"Missed what?" My eyes narrowed. "What is it you missed?"

"You not being able to figure it out is why you don't deserve my sister."

* * * *

Since neither Quinn nor Ashlyn would speak to me, or, as far as I knew, each other, I spent the last two weeks holed up in my office, drinking by myself once the workday was through. The pain I'd seen in Ashlyn's eyes that night still ripped at me. So did Quinn's last words, telling me how I didn't deserve her. But at least I got to see Ashlyn every day as she walked to the theater from Jessica's house behind the bar. A couple of times I even thought about following her, but in the end decided against it. The scene reminded me too much of the one where Andy stalks Caroline.

So I worked when I had to and drank when I didn't, conducting an odd experiment that might not make sense to anyone but me. And each night I drank, I wondered when it would happen—when I would hit that point where a taste for alcohol would turn into a craving and the destruction of my life and everyone around me. And yet the more I drank, the less I wanted to. But I forced it anyway. I had to find out if the bad parts of Michael had been passed down to me. Would I become like my father—a raging, abusive drunk—or had Ashlyn been right? Had my protective instincts made me like hers—a controlling, overbearing sonofabitch?

My skull nearly split in half when Babs bounded in my office on a Sunday morning, five days before opening night of the festival. She dropped a duffel bag none too gently on top of my stomach as I lay on the couch, nursing yet another hangover.

"Thought you might be running out of clean clothes, Michael."

I pushed the duffel onto the floor as I rose to sitting. Then I cradled my hammering head in my hands. "Stop calling me Michael."

"I will when you stop acting like him."

At least in oblivion, I had peace. Finally, I felt like I understood him.

Babs moved around the room, swiping empty beer bottles into a trash can she carried, making all kinds of noise as she went. "It doesn't have to be this way, you know…between you and her."

"Ashlyn needs to be free to make her own choices, live her own life." Because that's what she wanted, right? No interference?

"So that's it? You're just gonna offer yourself up as the martyr because you got a bum rap as a kid?"

I wasn't about to admit to Babs that I had only just discovered Michael had nothing to do with it. I couldn't see myself becoming an alcoholic, and Pritchard still being present in Phair more than proved I could control my violent impulses.

I grabbed a three-quarter-empty bottle of whiskey and thought about drinking it. "You know, your sarcasm really gets old sometimes."

"So does your stupidity." The bottle Babs dropped missed the trash and landed with a clink on the floor. Miraculously, it didn't break. She bent to pick it up. By the time she straightened, her entire demeanor had changed. "Life is about choices, Noah. You choose to drink, you choose not to. You choose to be a good person and do right by others, or you don't."

Choices was exactly where Babs was wrong. If I had a choice about falling in love, it sure wouldn't have been with my closest friend's sister. It was bad enough not being with the woman I loved. Not being able to talk about it with my best friend only made things worse.

With that realization, I took the bottle of whiskey into the bathroom and poured it down the sink. The stuff tasted like shit, anyway.

"Finally," Babs said. "Maybe now we can get some common sense around here."

Yeah, maybe we could.

"Do you want to talk about it?" she asked.

"There's nothing to talk about. I've learned my lesson. I can't always be in control."

CHAPTER NINETEEN

Ashlyn

Everything inside me hurt. My heart, my lungs, my ribs. Even the hair follicles of my skin ached. Having gone through heartbreak over Noah before, I thought I knew what it felt like. But what I'd experienced at seventeen had nothing on this.

As I walked from Jessica's house and headed to The Marshall Theater to watch one of the last rehearsals, I realized I had to give Noah credit. He'd been true to his word. According to Lucas, Noah had convinced the fire marshal to give the theater until after the festival to bring the electrical up to code. Even though the repairs couldn't be done without extensive work, it at least allowed for the theater to remain open during the critical time.

Noah had also secured volunteer firemen to be on the premises watching for signs and potential hazards during the festival for safety's sake. Even though his methods and motives with me were sometimes circumspect, Noah was a good man who cared about people. Like Andy Rich, his strongest characteristic had led to his downfall. I just hope I wasn't wrong for believing in redemption.

"Hey, Ash," Jess said, catching me as I made my way through the theater lobby. "Come check out the finished set."

I followed her backstage. Most of the props were a re-use of previous shows; the living room, Caroline's bedroom...Andy's office. My heart twisted, thinking about scenes that hadn't been scenes until they'd happened between Noah and me. But it was the bus stop—the symbol of the road less traveled—that caused my heart to stop beating. It was everything I'd pictured in my head. Vibrantly colored and larger than life, it represented choices—continue down the beaten path or carve your own way.

Stay.

Or go.

A grin spread across my face as I took it all in. It felt sincere, but also a little forced. "It's perfect."

"About Kyle..." Jess said. "Have you decided anything?"

She was referring to surveillance footage taken by Noah and Quinn that I'd told her all about. I still hadn't decided what to do—turn it over to the festival committee and let them deal with Kyle, or handle him myself. But after a morning of intense soul searching, I'd come closer to a decision.

"I'm going to face him after rehearsals."

"Atta girl," Jess said, grinning. As I turned to walk away, she caught me by the arm and added, "Hey, Ash, wait. I just want you to know I'm not worried. Whatever happens at the festival, to the theater, none of that's on you. And no one will blame you if it doesn't go a certain way."

I pulled her into a hug. "Thank you. And thank you for being here for me these last couple of weeks."

Her brow creased. "What about Noah? Are you going to try talking to him?"

I was surprised I hadn't run into him, especially considering the proximity of Jess's house to the Double Shot. But sometimes I could feel him watching me from the window of his office as I walked from her house to the theater. Somehow that gave me hope that one day soon he'd come around. So I answered her question as honestly as I could. "The stage has been set and the next lines are his. I want love or I want nothing. Noah knows where to find me…until I'm gone."

Excusing myself, I circled around to the front of the theater to see rehearsals were already underway. Other than a couple of quick e-mails back and forth in which I couldn't determine his tone, I hadn't communicated with Lucas since turning in my final draft. Now, hearing how cheerful he sounded as he gave direction led me to believe he was pleased with the finished product.

And he should be pleased.

Once I closed my eyes and listened to my words come alive in the inflection of voices, I realized this was definitely my most profound script yet.

I'd nailed it.

By the time six o'clock hit, the Marshall Theater Players had reached the pivotal scene—where Caroline's father shows up, offering her untold riches to do the right thing and marry the man he's chosen for her. Though she seems to struggle with her decision, in the end, the choice is easy. All the money and influence in the world can't give her the one thing Andy's love can—a life and love of her own choosing.

A familiar warmth eclipsed me as I sat in the last row of the orchestra seating level, watching the final act unfold. I would've known Noah's spicy clean scent anywhere. And though I didn't turn or acknowledge him in any way, I felt his hand pass over the back of my loose-hanging hair. He was here, watching the play. Watching my words come to life. Watching his community come together to form something brilliant.

And for the first time since leaving his house two weeks ago, I knew exactly what remained undone in spite of *his* choices.

Plans had changed, which caused me to look at my problems in a whole new way. I wanted Broadway and my name in lights, but I didn't *need* that.

But Noah needed Phair. He needed the big deal with the Cambridge Hotel to go through so he wouldn't lose investors, but it wasn't just that—he needed a place where he felt at home.

And Phair gave him what his family never could. A home.

The Marshall Theater had to succeed in the festival. And even with Kyle's threats to undermine the reviews, I single-handedly had the power to make that happen.

My inheritance.

If the Marshall Theater Players lost Best in Show, Broadway and my inheritance would slip through my fingers. But that didn't change the caveat to the contract

I'd signed with my father. If I didn't make a substantive career from writing by my twenty-fifth birthday—which was right around the corner—the funds in my trust would forfeit to the charity of my choice. And my charity of choice was The Marshall Theater. If I gave my inheritance to the theater, it would stay open. And the town, along with the Double Shot, would continue to thrive.

Just like Caroline, I was taking charge of my destiny. If Noah wouldn't accept my love, I could at least feel good in leaving him, and his town, this.

Still, I wasn't going to go down without a fight. But how? What could I do? A last-minute trip to the batting cage was exactly what I needed to get my head together and put my plan in place.

* * * *

Still sweaty from smacking softballs for a good hour at the batting cages, I pulled up to Kyle Pritchard's RV. I honked my horn once, grabbed the flash drive from the console, then stood outside the car. Movement from inside the trailer caught my eye. Kyle was home. I quickly looked around me. Being a Sunday, the lot was nearly empty. Weekenders had packed up and gone home. A late summer breeze rustled the leaves that still hung tight to oak trees, and I wondered where Noah had hidden the cameras.

The door to the RV opened and Kyle Pritchard stepped out, holding a glass of red wine. A smile slowly curved his thin lips, and I knew exactly what he was thinking.

"Better late than never, I suppose," he said.

The bastard actually thought I'd come to sleep with him.

"I have something for you." I handed over the flash drive. "Don't worry, you can keep that one. I have plenty of copies."

Kyle took the flash drive from my hand as I held up my phone and played the video Noah and Quinn had taken of Kyle threatening me. His jaw went slack and his color faded as the scene played out. When it was over, I switched off the phone.

"So here's how this works, Kyle. I don't need to play dirty to get what I want. So you do what you feel compelled to during the festival. My writing talent will speak for itself. I only ask that you judge fair. But I'm guessing I wasn't the only underage girl you tried to take. So if I ever hear of you sexually harassing or sexually assaulting another girl for as long as you live, I swear to God I won't stop until every major media outlet and judge on a bench has seen this video. And I can guarantee the civil and criminal justice system won't give a damn your last name is Pritchard. I have eyes and ears everywhere, Kyle. I'm always watching."

Kyle's lip curled up and I saw pure hatred in his eyes. But he was a man who'd finally learned when to talk and when to listen. Slowly, he turned and walked back into his trailer.

My phone vibrated with a text as I ducked back into my car.

It was from Noah.

Nicely done.

I couldn't help but smile and think this day might not have happened—the day I reclaimed the power I'd lost— if he hadn't interfered.

CHAPTER TWENTY

Noah

Phair was as alive as I'd ever seen it. Street vendors and shopkeepers sold souvenirs, food, and beer. The atmosphere hummed with electricity as actors in full costume and make-up engaged citizens on the street, acting out scenes or comedic bits. Today was the grand opening of The Phair Theater Festival, and the entire town was humming.

Inside The Marshall Theater, the mood was more subdued. Now that everyone knew The Marshall was likely to be closed down, the tension was as thick as a Texas rib-eye. For all anyone knew, this could be the last performance ever played on this stage.

At least Kyle Pritchard was no longer a threat. After Ashlyn's little visit, he'd packed up his RV and headed out of town. I'd been so proud of her the day she'd stuck up for herself with Pritchard. It had taken everything I had not to follow her out there. To protect her. But she'd needed to face him herself. And I'd needed to let her fight her own battles. On her own terms.

Tonight, though, I was the one about to take a risk.

What I had to do was for Ashlyn and me. No one else. Not Lucas, not the town, not Quinn, or even Babs. I loved Ashlyn, and by the time the evening was over, everyone would know how much.

But God, I hated feeling this way. I'd never been unsure of anything like I was now, never cared about a woman enough to put it all out there. But no matter how it played, Ashlyn was worth the fight.

My mind blanked the moment she walked through the backstage door, headed toward her usual spot on the aisle at the middle of the orchestra-level seating. She took her seat, then I followed to sit next to her.

When I unbuttoned my sport coat and sat down beside her, she did a double-take.

"Hi," she said, skittishly meeting my eyes. I got the sense she wasn't nervous about the play, but rather over this first face-to-face meeting since she left me three weeks ago.

My eyes dropped to her dress, the same shade of blue as her eyes during sex. The deep V in the front showed just enough to be intriguing. It only helped that Ashlyn had the perfect kind of body worth showing off. "Nice dress."

She tried to hide the little smile that played at the corner of her lips. "Stop staring at my breasts, Noah."

If it'd been anyone but her, I might have taken her order seriously. Instead, I shrugged and said, "I wouldn't be a man if I didn't at least look," then sneaked another peek.

The lights slowly dimmed and the play began. As one scene flowed into another, sitting next to Ashlyn became pure hell. It felt like every line in every scene was being spoken to me. And when it came time for that pivotal love scene, the one where Caroline went to Andy's office wearing his coat, I thought I'd jump out of my skin. Then Ashlyn's hand inched over beneath the arm rest to squeeze the inside of my thigh.

For the rest of the play, she let me hold her hand, pulling away only at the end. That's when Andy took Caroline to the bus stop where they first met, intent on sending her back home. But at the end of the play, Andy Rich and Caroline got their happy ending. I just hoped Ashlyn and I would, too.

As the curtain closed on *Midnight in Summer,* from the corner of my eye, I saw Haywire motion me to the front. That's when Lucas Marshall took the stage.

"If everyone could remain seated for a moment, we have a special guest."

I turned to Ashlyn, took her face in my hands, and planted a quick kiss on her unsuspecting lips. Then, buttoning my sport coat as I went, I climbed the stage.

"Ladies and gentlemen," Lucas said, gesturing to me, "The real Andy Rich."

After a few awkward catcalls from my personal cheering squad, I finally spoke. "My name's not Andy Rich, but I was the inspiration for his character. And I have something I want to say to the real Caroline."

Haywire pointed the spotlight so that it shined directly down on Ashlyn. Surprised and unsure what to do, she ducked down a little into her seat, and wouldn't meet my gaze with hers.

Not a good sign.

But I had to do this anyway. She'd channeled her inner Caroline before. Now was my turn to channel my inner Andy Rich.

"Ashlyn, I've known you half my life, and have loved you almost as long."

Something caught in my throat. The crowd murmured, and I held up a hand, asking for silence.

Noticing how her body language shifted, how she straightened, taller, I took that as a sign to push on. I sucked in a breath and continued. "These last few weeks without you have been miserable. But you know something? They made me figure a few things out."

Finally, she brought her chin back up. Looked straight at the stage. And our eyes locked. In my field of vision, the audience of five thousand seemed to fade into the woodwork of the limestone theater, leaving only Ashlyn and me.

I waited, knowing I needed to speak, but needing her to meet me at least part way. Nothing. Not even a hint of a smile. And then I saw it. A slight lifting of her right eyebrow.

"Yes, I can definitely be the Patron Saint of Assholes," I said. "I can be overprotective and controlling and arrogant. And I have a temper. But I'm not my father. And I'm not *your* father."

Odd, how silence seemed to travel. Five thousand theater-goers filled the room, yet I could hear my own ragged breath.

"But most importantly, Ashlyn, you need to know I didn't champion for you to come to Phair so I could save you. That's the excuse I'd given myself. But in the back of my mind, I always knew the truth. I did it so you could save me."

A chorus of *aahhhs* echoed. Dusty, looking dapper in a tailored blazer and carrying two dozen red roses, made his way down the aisle, stopping at her row. When he held his hand out to her, she turned to him, but made no move to get up. Her face turned away from me so I couldn't read her expression.

Oh, God, it was over. She was done. I'd screwed up too badly by finking on her to her brother. Spying on her when she was with Pritchard.

Seconds felt like lifetimes before she stood. My heart skipped a beat, then another. Was she headed out the door, straight for Broadway, or would she come to me? To us?

Dusty thrust the flowers toward her. And I waited. Letting her take control. Slowly, her hand reached out. Slowly, she took the flowers. Slowly, she placed her hand in the crook of his elbow he offered her.

Then allowed him to escort her down the aisle, to me. That's when I finally exhaled. And jumped down from the stage to meet her halfway.

Tears glittered her eyes. When she spoke, her voice was thin and reedy. "Noah, what are you doing?"

"I love you, Ashlyn. But I won't apologize for who I am. I won't say I'm sorry for wanting to be the person who always has your back. Because I love you. I love you more than my company, this theater, this town, or even my best friend. I'd give all that up for you. If you'll marry me, I promise I'll spend the rest of my life privileged to be your muse."

Dusty handed over the ring. I slipped a six carat, emerald-cut canary on her finger, waiting for that all important yes. But she was hell-bent on making me sweat it out.

"You hear me when I don't think you're listening," she said, wiping away her tears. "You know what I need when I'm too proud to ask. All the things I thought I hated are what I love most about you, Noah. Because you carried me until I was strong enough to stand."

And as Ashlyn finally said yes, I saw Quinn stand and clap. In laying my heart bare for everyone to see, I'd finally figured out what it was that made me deserve his sister. Vulnerability.

* * * *

Epilogue

Eight weeks later…

Ashlyn

Sitting on the sun porch at Noah's house, I hit the end button on my phone and laid it down on the pillow beside me. A tingly feeling zipped through my extremities.

I'd sold my script.

Only, *Midnight in Summer* wasn't going to be a Broadway smash. Even after Noah's heart-felt marriage proposal, or probably because of it, the Marshall Theater Players had taken runner-up in the Phair Theater Festival. But that didn't dampen interest in my script. Instead, it had gone to a major movie studio for a cool seven figures—which was good, considering my father's lawyers had followed through with the paperwork and legally divested me of my inheritance. That money was now fattening The Marshall Theater bank account. I'd come out of my time writing plays for Lucas dead broke, with only a run-down loveseat and a borrowed beanbag to my name.

But I had Noah.

Still wearing his shirt and loose-fitting tie he'd worn to the Cambridge Hotels ground-breaking ceremony earlier in the morning, Noah entered carrying a bottle of champagne and two glasses.

"Is it celebration time?" he asked.

I grinned. "I'll get the contract to sign in a few days."

"Congratulations, Wheels." His face split into a grin and he enfolded me in his arms, champagne bottle and glasses clinking together behind my back. "What happens now? Do we go to LA?"

"What if I told you LA is coming to us in twelve weeks?"

"I'd say that's great timing. With the theater closed for renovation, maybe some of the actors will find replacement work."

"But here's the thing, Noah. Now that I'm a professional writer, I really need to consider my image. The Training Wheels thing *has* to go."

He held out the bottle of champagne. "Tell you what. If you can drink this whole bottle without getting drunk, I'll stop calling you Wheels."

"Find me anyone who can drink a bottle of champagne and not get drunk."

"That's the deal. Take it or leave it."

If he wasn't going to play fair, neither would I. A third of the bottle spilled to the floor when the cork popped. When I raised my arms, Noah pulled my shirt up and tossed it aside. He licked the bubbly from between my breasts when I poured, lapped it from my navel. Already we were half a bottle down.

"That's cheating," he said, removing his shirt and tie. But when I rose up again and poured the drink on his chest, then ran my tongue over his body, he lost all interest in complaining.

And then his lips were on mine. His fingers entwined through my hair.

"How about we make a deal," Noah said. "I'll stop calling you Training Wheels if you run away with me next weekend."

"And if I do, what will you call me then?"

"Mrs. Blake."

I grinned, my heart soaring as high as the blue Texas sky. "Well played, Mr. Blake. You've got yourself a deal."

ABOUT THE AUTHOR

When she's not writing, Tracy is a chauffeur, a maid, a short-order cook, a coach, a psychic/intuitive who always finds what her husband loses, a yoga nut, a mango margarita connoisseur, and a really bad dancer. She currently writes for Entangled Publishing's Indulgence imprint.

ACKNOWLEDGEMENTS

Though there may be only one name in the byline of this book, no author makes it to publication alone. I owe these people more gratitude than any words can express.

Many thanks goes to the professionals at Entangled Publishing for bringing the first edition of this novel to life. To the Lit Girls for always being in my corner— Marty Tidwell, Jessica Davidson, Beatriz Terrazas, Rebecca Reed, Kym Matthews, Misa Ramirez, Jill Wilson, Kim Quinton, Mary Duncanson, and Wendy Watson. I am humbled to be among such a fantastic group of writers. Special thanks goes to Misa Ramirez and Kym Matthews. If it weren't for the insurmountable peer pressure and the plotting session the two of you forced on me, this book would not have been thought up much less contracted and written. I will forever be grateful.

To all the writers of NT-RWA and DFW Writers Workshop: your feedback and your fellowship over the years made learning the craft and the business slightly less daunting and far less lonely.

To my dear friend Daryle McGinnis: thank you for your smart-ass critiques, your careful attention to logic, and for telling me long ago the word "crotch" should never ever be used in a sexy scene. Also, I left "had" in just for you.

Thanks to my good friend, Sally Miller. Your proofreading skills are epic and I wouldn't have made my deadline without you.

To Ty, my real-life hero: thanks for bank-rolling me, for rarely complaining, and for never doubting. To Taylor and Dylan, for making it possible to have it all.